AFTER SUMMER

Nick Earls

WALKER BOOKS
AND SUBSIDIARIES
LONDON · BOSTON · SYDNEY · AUCKLAND

First published in Great Britain 2004 by Walker Books Ltd
87 Vauxhall Walk, London SE11 5HJ

2 4 6 8 10 9 7 5 3 1

Text © 1996 Nick Earls
Cover photograph © Anne Ackermann/Getty Images

This book has been typeset in Optima

Printed in Great Britain by Cox & Wyman Ltd, Reading, Berkshire

British Library Cataloguing in Publication Data:
a catalogue record for this book is
available from the British Library

ISBN 1-84428-630-4

www.walkerbooks.co.uk

Acknowledgments

There are a number of people I would like to thank, either for their direct assistance or for allowing me, on occasions, to borrow things from our pasts:

Noel Box, without whom Len Boit would have been a fictional character.

My mother, who may have said several quotable mother things.

My cousin Mark, whose cross-dressing days appear to be long behind him.

Paul, who has a unique ability with the pumpkin.

Sally Bick, then working at TEPA, for useful advice concerning tertiary entrance (at this point it is only reasonable to state that any departures from or errors in connection with the actual contemporary procedures for tertiary entrance in Queensland are the responsibility of the author, who is at times prone to handling advice clumsily and without due regard).

Robyn and Leonie, for getting this started, and keeping it going.

1135391

1

This begins in January, and January is okay. It begins like December as though their join is seamless. Sometimes as though the bright days of summer will last forever.

But the end of January is the end of the known world. This is when I stand at the edge. It's been easy till now, relatively. I've had a new school year to face each January, but not this year. School is over, so there is not the usual symmetry about the holidays. The feeling of days leading up to Christmas and New Year and then away. Across the slow heat-heavy weeks of January and back to school.

This January I'm waiting for my offer, waiting for the code that will tell me what happens next. Waiting.

It's as though the future is held here. Held at bay, held at more than arm's length. Held just beyond my reach all the long days of summer. And the waiting is everywhere, in the rhythm of waves and winds, in the familiar lights and sounds of the coastal summer, in the sun rising over the sea and settling through an orange sky into the Glasshouse Mountains. The impossible days and nights of a suspended world.

It's hard not to think about the day I'm waiting for.

The twentieth of January. Seventeen days from today. On the twentieth of January it all comes out in the paper and I'll be there with the others from school around midnight at Newspaper House, the way the uni students do in December. I'll head down from the coast and I'll meet the others and we'll buy a paper and then we'll all know. I'll go to bed knowing, and in the morning everyone will know; everyone who bothers to look for my name and work out the code — everyone who's ever known me, expected things from me, expected me to make it. They'll know right then whether I have, or not. And then it will come in the mail. A few days later maybe, and just the way that phone bills come, and reminders from the dentist, and my mother's medical journals. Just as unannounced, just as unspecial, wound in a bundle with a rubber band or wrapped in plastic if it looks like rain. One envelope, a few sheets of paper, the definite offer in writing. And if the newspaper says I made it I still won't believe it till I see the letter. If the newspaper says I didn't, then I won't want the letter.

I should stop thinking of it as though it's weeks of sensory deprivation leading up to an execution. I should stop thinking of it and get a life.

The waves change with changes in the weather far out to sea, storms and cyclones and winds, and the first of January blew in a forest of red weed and a fleet of blue box jellyfish, and the second blew them away again. Whatever it's like I go to the beach early because I'm in the habit of it. It's the best time. On all but the worst days I swim, and my body is still warm and creased with sleep and the first cold wave always comes as a shock.

I'm facing the house when I look back at the shore,

8

the fibro beach house lit up white by the sun, the white plastic chairs on the long veranda, the unbleached calico curtains through the locked sliding glass doors, my mother asleep inside. My mother who was very clear with her *This is my holiday too you know and I don't expect to be woken before nine.* Said as a joke, but worth remembering anyway. *And I expect to have my breakfast brought to me in bed when I call for it.* She said that too. Yeah, so do I, I remember telling her; I wonder who'll bring it to us. So she makes her own breakfast, and takes it back there on a tray every day, and I can hear her swearing as she manoeuvres around among the crumbs afterwards, trying to read a novel.

This is a house I have known all my life, and each summer spent in it is a variation on the same routine. My mother with her same holiday expectations of doing nothing for weeks, but gardening by the third day and cleaning out leaves from the gutters because *it's not as though anyone else will ever do it. It's not as though anyone else would even notice.* Meaning my father.

Each year I come up here and the sliding door opens and the house smells of seagrass matting just the way I know it will, that trapped musty smell that it accumulates in just a few warm days. And there's the same Caloundra furniture, the seventies Brisbane lounge suite where anyone who sits down is taken prisoner by the sagging upholstery, the underfilled bean bags covered in bedroom curtains from so long ago I can't remember them as curtains, the pine dining table with its bench seats and the teeth marks of infants, including perhaps my own. And on the wall the same macrame owl with mis-matched shells for eyes. There is nothing like this place.

I swim in the sea right in front of the house. I catch waves that take me in a straight line right back towards the bright white fibro. This is the part of every holiday least like life in a flat in the city. Waves at the door. Even if there are better waves to the north at Dicky Beach or south at Kings, I usually swim here. These waves are mine.

This morning the waves aren't great but they're okay, coming in in unspectacular threes and fours with long spaces between. I float and I look out to sea in case there's anything better out there, but there isn't, so then I set off on whatever's passing.

I'm built for this, made into a shape with this in mind, my light streamlined body — describing it in terms of its aerodynamics is the kindest way to deal with fifty-five kilos stretched across a 178-centimetre frame — my arms looped under me like the runners on a sled. And I stay on the wave all the way in. All the way till there is no wave and it fades to nothing and drops out from under me. Some days when the surf is right it takes me all the way till I hit sand with the tip of my shoulder or the bony points of my pelvis and I flip or roll and the wave slips back and I'm on the beach. On the beach with sand down my togs and in my hair and in my mouth, and no one else catches waves this way. But then maybe no one else is built with a chest like a bird cage, a body shape not often found desirable, that feels quite undesirable when I'm beached and I'm all ribs and limbs and none of my angles are turned in any way gracefully. I have assumed that I am more likely to be desired for my wit and intellect, and possibly only in winter when I can hide the rest in jumpers. But it's a body that catches waves in a way the more conventionally shaped can only envy. *A body you'll grow into*, my mother sometimes says as a joke. A body I'll never grow used to.

But there's more to you than that, my mother says. *What about that girl Juliet, the one who was in the play with you?* What about her? We did the play, we kissed in the school play and it all lingers in my mind like a relationship. The problem was it was probably only ever in my mind. I can see her even now, that look, the last look she ever gave me, telling me about a school dance as though we were arranging to meet there. I went but I didn't see her. I haven't seen her since. All I have left is the fifteen episodes of our 'relationship', thirteen rehearsals and two performances, and the story I wrote two days later when she was all I could think about. The story I showed my mother in a moment of weakness, not realising of course how much she would like it. *It's beautiful*, she said. *It's beautiful.* And she kept saying it as though it was some miracle. *It's beautiful, and nobody dies. You wrote this story and nobody dies. There's no blood at all. No weapons, no heavy machinery, no mutilation. It's so unlike you.*

She started making copies and I took this for the grim sign that it was. At least one copy changed hands at a parent-teacher night and my English teacher took me aside the next day and told me it should be in the school magazine. I told him that as I was one of the editors I thought this would be inappropriate and he told me, *There's a time and a place for modesty*, and he seemed to have made up his mind that this was neither. I told him that the girl in the story was based on the daughter of my maths teacher, Mr Koh, and that the story was based on the school play and I was really

11

rather annoyed with my mother for circulating it. He said that it was a beautiful story and that my mother was right to be proud and that he was sure people would accept it as a work of fiction if that's what we told them it was. I said that in many respects, or at least in some, it was actually fiction, but I was concerned about how Mr Koh would feel. He looked at me earnestly with his rumpled middle-aged face and his fading grey eyes and he said again that it was a beautiful story, and he was sure Mr Koh would see it that way too. I knew I was losing. After this he brought me his poetry, and took notes when I gave my opinion. I knew I should never have written that story.

And it went in the school magazine and won the literary competition and it gave me a fleeting clandestine kind of fame, but fame only among the sort of people who had already seen the play and who would think a story in which almost nothing happens can still have credibility. For the socially important, the several acts of this tiny drama passed completely unnoticed.

Maybe Juliet saw it but whether she did or she didn't I haven't seen her since. Not at any dance, not at schoolies' week after our exams, not at all.

I catch a wave. And it's as though I'm passing through this summer in a bubble. Vaguely detached and drifting. I'm not even thinking about the wave. I'm observing but not participating, squandering these counting-down days, willing January to come to an end, willing it not to.

There are people out now, jogging, walking dogs without leashes despite the signs, a girl in the surf nearby. I notice her as I turn and she's on a wave, lifting herself to a standing position on her board. And the sun is partly behind her, reflecting off the water so I don't see her well. Tanned legs balanced perfectly and comfortably, sun-bleached hair in a wet pony tail, the bare elegant muscles of her shoulders and back. This is the last thing I need, to be floating around staring into the sun at some girl I can't even see properly. I should go home and write a story about it and please my mother.

One more wave and I'll go in. There's always the temptation to wait for a really good wave to finish with but I know it won't come today. So I take the next one and I head for the showers. This is all part of the routine, right down to the seventy cents I've wrapped in my towel to buy the *Courier-Mail*.

On these mornings my brain doesn't work till it's woken by the surf, so I need the routine. This, my mother says, is a habit of my father's, and hence not highly regarded. My mother claims to despise routines, though she will inevitably enact one within the next few hours when she makes her breakfast. *It's not a routine*, she'll say if I question her. *It's just something I enjoy doing, so why shouldn't I do it every day?*

At the newsagent in Seaview Terrace I buy the paper, like every other morning, and I walk home with my towel around my shoulders and let myself in with the key I have left in one of the sandshoes lying near the door. The house is dark inside and still cool, my mother almost certainly still asleep.

2

I read the paper. I consume the silent breakfast I am now used to. Not the high speed breakfast of home, my mother rushing to be ready for work and me for school. The holiday breakfast when no one else is awake and there's just the sound of the sea out the back and the scraping of the knife on the toast and the boiling of the jug.

I take my tea and toast to the table and read the paper but this is summer and no one around here is making news. The real stories are in other countries.

So what do I do now? I've finished the paper and there's no one around. I've finished the books on the bookshelves. This is clearly a test of my abilities as a holiday-maker, my ability to relax. I hear my mother turn over in bed, but in the way sleeping people do, not like someone waking up.

I could go for another swim but the surf is no good. I could go next door but I don't hear anyone up yet, and I can usually hear Len clattering a few things around in the kitchen if he's making breakfast.

I decide to sleep. I try to tell myself this is fine, that this is a perfectly reasonable thing to do on a holiday and it doesn't indicate that I've run out of even vaguely

14

productive activities. I try to convince myself that this is a choice, that I actually want to go back to sleep.

I lie on a bean bag, on cartoon palm trees with their cartoon monkeys in fezes and waistcoats and slippers turned up at the toes. Maybe this is a movie I liked, so my mother bought the curtains for my room. I don't recall. I can remember being so bored in *Fantasia* that I cried, but I don't remember the monkey cartoon. Maybe it was only ever just a curtain. I don't know.

The curtains in my dream are brown, violent geometric brown and burnt orange. A cyclone is beginning. My parents stand on the brown-tiled balcony, looking down Pumicestone Passage, over Bribie Island and out to sea. My mother, who is in the late stages of pregnancy, has both her hands on the white railing. My father has one hand on her right shoulder, tenderly. (This is after all a dream, and it has its own rules.)

My mother's hand holds an envelope, my tertiary entrance offer. She seems unaware of it, even though it's my whole future. The wind gusts. The free end of the envelope flaps against the railings, as though it doesn't matter at all, as though it's up to the wind now, and the wind doesn't care.

I'm at a window. At the huge window along the side of Mayne Hall at uni with my mouth sucked against the glass in a pool of steam, my uvula waggling at the back of my throat as the air moves out in a scream that goes nowhere. There are thousands of people in the hall for orientation, thousands of people and, far up the back, one empty seat. I read the Vice Chancellor's lips as they say, *Well if everyone's here we'll begin*, and everyone shrugs their shoulders and he does begin and I'm not there.

I'm in a bubble. In a bubble, turning over and over in blind warm fluid and my mother holds the envelope in one hand and doesn't even know. I'm in an advanced stage of intrauterine life and already the future is beyond my grasp, beyond my tiny waxy see-through fingers, squeezing and relaxing pointlessly in the fluid.

And there are monkeys around me. Monkeys in fezes and waistcoats and slippers turned up at the toes and they're dancing. Dancing for hours and hours to the same insistent rhythm section with an occasional sax solo from a crocodile in dark glasses. Hours and hours of the same repetitive monotonous pointless steps and the same inane smiles with the background switching from homogeneous pink to homogeneous blue and back again every couple of bars.

Fantasia.

I think I'm going to cry.

Lying there with your mouth open catching flies, my mother says when I wake.

She is making breakfast. No one has brought it to her in bed.

Like your cousin, she says. *Do you remember Mark when he was young? When he was three maybe and that whole summer he'd want to stay up late and be part of everything and every night he'd sit in a bean bag and pass out.*

He is now fourteen but he will always be trapped by his aunt's memories of the summer he wanted to wear a woman's black silk blouse all the time. The summer when he could only go to the toilet with the door open while he sat there swinging his legs and singing. It was a small house and its toilet was a strangely proportioned room that seemed to deliver its every sound to every other part of the house, but only when the door was open. We were a close family that summer, and we had no choice but to know intimately every sound Mark made in there.

This is what my mother is telling me. This is the joke. Not merely that my mouth happened to be open because I fell asleep half sitting up on a bean bag, but that this implies I am a juvenile cross-dresser who attends to very personal needs in public.

I've finished my book, she says, as though this means her plan of going back to bed with her breakfast is ruined. *Is there anything in the paper?*

Not really.

When will your thing be coming out? The offer.

A couple of weeks or so. A few weeks.

Today neither of us wants this conversation. She picks up the front section of the paper and manages not to tell me it doesn't matter really. She begins to eat her toast and I know she wants to tell me that tertiary offers are no reflection of a person's worth, that there is much more to a person than a numerical score and a coded offer, but even she knows that every time she tries to convince us both of this she sounds like a self-help book that is in reality a no-help book. Next, in the conversation we are not having today, I would be told of the many joys ahead, whatever the outcome. I would be told again about her days at uni, the great times she had, the balls, the late nights, horrendous medical student practical jokes, the man who accidentally threw a liver out of the window of the anatomy lab because someone ducked, the clinical tutorial when people loaded her pockets with condoms and she pulled out her stethoscope and they flew everywhere. *Right in front of the Professor of Medicine.* And so on.

This is supposed to help me, to promise me bright moments, but what if I don't have them? What if it doesn't work out this way? What if I end up making the wrong friends early on and behave like a complete dork and study hard and end up with an honours degree by accident and the people who have the fun don't speak to me, don't even know I exist? It seems distinctly possible that the cool people will find each other early and I'll be left with the losers. That I will spend my glorious undergraduate days not in the company of heroes, but with people who never muss a tute, never miss a lecture, never go out at night, bring packed lunches instead of hanging out wherever it is you're supposed to hang out, trip over condom vending machines and cause themselves trivial injuries instead of knocking off a handful for a legendary prank or two, and don't even have the social skills to judge when to blow their noses. *Revenge of the Nerds* part five and I'm the Nerd King. Not the biggest nerd, but the best a nerd can ever aspire to. An unfortunate organism that only a rude quirk of fate prevented from having a human life. Another one of those times when a really important line was drawn, and I was damn close.

Today, we don't have this conversation. Today we side-step the conversation, and I jump right to the failing part. I am growing used to this now. I expect that when I turn up at uni, whatever course I end up doing, this will have become so much a part of me that I shall seek out the nerds early, and live as one of them.

Perhaps I should tell my mother now, and attempt to lessen the inevitable later pain.

5

I hear feet on the steps outside. The unhurried heavy feet of Len Boit.

G'day young Alex, he says when his head appears over the edge of the veranda. *Fancy a frame or two?*

His right hand vigorously works an imaginary cue while his face realigns its wrinkles to make his one open eye seem very large as it takes aim at a distant pocket. This, for a moment, might look like a clever caricature of a pool player, but it is in fact the very way Len plays every shot. Same enthusiastic cue work, same intimidating cycloptic aim.

Son, I could make those balls talk once, he told me a year or two ago.

Perhaps he could, though most of us would settle for hitting them into the pockets.

It's all bloody trigonometry and a good eye, he said. *That's all it is.*

And the eye was more than apparent, and when it came to the trigonometry I knew the maths but for me it always seemed easier on the page.

The balls are already racked when we get to Len's place. We chalk our regular cues with the solemnity of duellists. As the guest it is the custom that I break first.

With characteristic caution, Len says after my shot as he sizes up his options, *young Alex breaks and gives nothing away.*

So he mirrors the shot, sending the cue ball down and back and glancing one ball on the way. I make the first mistake. A slight misjudgment and the cue ball ricochets into the pack. Len pots the ten and the twelve, and I don't usually win from here. Today is no exception. He takes the second frame too, but it's closer, and he tells me he should be heading off to the Home.

The Home is a place where Len uses his natural gregariousness and yarn-spinning rhyme-turning talents to best effect, at least a couple of times a week. The way he tells it, he gets a few of the old blokes together on the veranda and he hands around a six-pack and they talk about the old days.

He recites a selection of the Classics, by which he means Banjo Paterson, Henry Lawson and maybe even some Steele Rudd, and he throws in a few of his own. He stands with the poem typed on a sheet of paper which he holds a long way out in front of him and he tilts his head a little to look through the right part of his glasses, fiddles with the glasses with his free hand, takes a deep breath and he's off, with a booming voice that could throw a poem several streets if he wanted it to, but with a soft touch when it counts. And sometimes he works bloody hard for that rhyme, shortening words with apostrophes and imposing a challenging meter, but he makes it. I've heard him do it on our front steps and on our veranda, and I bet they love him at the nursing home. He covers all the big topics: love, war (specialising in the Siege of Tobruk), the old days, neighbourhood events.

Since I won the school poetry competition three years ago, a bundle of Len's latest poems has been waiting for me when I arrive at the coast each summer. Even though I've written little poetry since and entered only the prose section of the competition this year, I think he still views me as a poet at heart, or at least as one of his more discerning listeners. It doesn't bother him that our styles are very different. He comes over as soon as he sees we're up here and he says, *Now, young Alex, you've got a bit of an interest in poetry*, and he straightens his pages, sets his glasses at a determined, poetic angle and begins.

He's off to the Home today with a new poem he's pleased with. He read it to me yesterday and he says it'll go well with 'The Man from Ironbark', and he hasn't done that one for a while. He packs them into his briefcase with a few others, and heads off like a man who knows he's got a hit on his hands, whistling as he shuts the car door.

Today there's no cricket to watch on TV and outside it's turning into a cruel kind of heat. I can hear people at the beach, the noise of children's voices over the sound of the breaking waves. I go home and pour myself water.

I look among the books for something to read, but the bookshelves are just a strange museum for bad paperbacks, local histories, guide books, maps, books that turned up here in summer and stayed. Books from old Anglo-Irish relatives, sent as Christmas presents. '1001 Activities for Rainy Days', designed to alleviate the boredom of English summer holidays. But most of the activities require a ready store of chestnuts or an acorn and six pins or sycamore leaves of several different hues. Or could only marginally be classified as activities. For example, 'Growing a Mustard and Cress Garden', which involves moist cotton, the appropriate seed and at least ten days expectant waiting. But I'm not good at waiting.

I also find my Caloundra Library card.

After lunch I strap on my bike helmet, tuck the card into my wallet and ride. The bike helmet is red-orange in colour, a choice agreed upon by my parents when it was bought for me, so I can efficiently signal the danger I represent. When it's on my head I look like a big Redhead match, and whatever I'm signalling, I don't think it's danger. Cars pass, blowing hot exhaust at me, and I am beginning to wonder about my enthusiasm for books.

The library, though, will be air-conditioned, and I can stay there a while. And who knows what might happen there.

This is the recurring senseless dream of bumping into someone young, female and desirable in any public place. This afternoon, for instance, among the Fiction shelves. Striking up a conversation. Revealing myself to be clever, funny and equally desirable, even though I often forget to take off the bike helmet and manage to look like a cross between a Redhead match and a complete dickhead.

What happens after this I don't know. It depends at least partly on her. I don't know what she has in mind.

All I know is she is young, female and desirable, and we like the same books. Or at least authors with alphabetically adjacent names.

But the library isn't like this, needless to say. Even when I'm included, the average age of the browsers is over sixty. Over in Fiction no one talks to me, and I talk to no one. This is mutually suitable.

My bike helmet is outside, chained up with my bike, but with the sweat of the ride my hair has now, I suspect, taken on the internal dimensions of the bike helmet anyway. I do not, at present, feel desirable. I do not think it likely that anyone could provoke me to conversation. So any glorious babe opportunity would slip through my fingers even if came my way.

It does not.

Nor has it on many occasions, not without the aid of a script and thirteen rehearsals and two performances. And I didn't exactly win that one either, I just re-shaped it into a more appealing fiction. Made just a little more of the eyes, the words than might have been there. Maybe. Took almost nothing and turned it into a range of convoluted, contradictory theories that have her wanting me, forgetting me, rejecting me or waiting for the call that I'm not brave enough to make. She is, after all, my maths teacher's daughter.

I have a fantasy that she holidays at Caloundra.

This is ridiculous. Ridiculous. Unfortunately I think I say this out loud. Ridiculous. So now I am the unspeakable nerd with a head shaped like a bike helmet standing in Fiction talking to himself. This is not good. Sometimes I think I've suffered from going to a single-sex school.

I go to the exit with the couple of books I have

already chosen. I check them out and leave. I ride home. Ridiculous. No one holidays at Caloundra. No one that desirable, not even if their father is a maths teacher. She's probably closer to Noosa, if she's anywhere on the coast. I can see her at Noosa, not out of place there at all.

I go for a swim because I am hot and because I want to change the shape of my head.

Afterwards, I sit on the veranda reading one of the books. The sun is behind me and the afternoon becomes evening and I hardly notice.

At the end of a chapter I look up and out through the pandanus trees, out at the sea. Far off, near the horizon, a long, low, red container ship begins the turn that will lead it into Brisbane. Closer, the girl is surfing again. The girl from this morning. Her body golden in the late light.

I find my towel and I go down to the beach.

She has gone.

THE POEM ABOUT THE WATCHER (notes)

So I am a watcher now.
And she a perfect form. She is gold, hot pouring gold
pouring down into the sea.
And she moves with the grace of a dolphin. As though
there are no angles, only curves, arcs, circles.
About this I can write a poem. And show it to no one.
About the magic light, the cut water, the riven ridden
wave.
This impossible sea creature, who comes and goes.
Through the water, through the sun.
Changing shape, changing, but no closer than art.
So the poem is about the idea, and the idea is mine.
Even in the empty sea.

My mother says, *Let's go out for dinner. You've really been festering today. You need to get out.*

We go to one of the Chinese restaurants in the main street.

I tell her I'm not festering. That I've been doing almost the same things she has, that the only difference in our days was she didn't get whipped two nothing at pool by Len Boit.

The only difference, essentially.

I keep the notes for the poem in my room. Folded and in my underwear drawer. They will be safe here, while I decide whether or not they will become something.

While I don't imagine my mother has been drafting poetry and storing it with underwear, I don't feel inclined to identify this as another differing part of our days.

We sit next to the tank with the trussed-up lobsters and our spring rolls don't take long.

So, good holiday then? my mother says, but in a faintly mocking tone, as though I'm still festering despite her good intentions.

Yeah, fine. Fine. What about you?

Great. Perfect. Very relaxing. A long pause to eat the last of her spring roll and lick the dribble of sweet and sour sauce from her thumb. *Get any good books out of the library today?*

Yeah, yeah. I've only started one, but it's okay. You'd hate it, but it's okay. Not a holiday read, really. More suited to the questioning, festering kind of reader. Not a book to crumb a bed up with. Not a book to fall asleep under while you're reading in bed.

I don't fall asleep when I'm reading in bed.

I've seen your light on, very late. Some nights I hear the book hit the floor.

It's better if it hits the floor. That way I don't roll on it in my sleep. They're not comfortable things to sleep on.

The Mongolian Lamb arrives, spitting on the thick metal plate.

Must have been a tough day for you, my mother says. *No cricket I mean. Six extra hours to kill. It's not easy, in a miserable place like this.*

I managed. A few swims, a few sleeps, a bit of a read.

A perfect lazy day then.

Perfect.

Do you want any of your friends to come up? You could have someone up for a couple of days if you wanted.

I think they're all doing other things at the moment. On holiday or doing things that mean they're stuck in Brisbane. We'll be back there soon anyway.

That's right. This all comes to an end, doesn't it? Back to Brisbane, back to work. What are you going to do when I'm back at work?

Watch cricket I suppose. So it'll be exactly the same as here, except the TV'll be bigger. I'll hardly notice I'm anywhere different.

She laughs.

I'll catch up with a few people, I tell her. Play some tennis maybe, head into town for a movie or two. I'll do things. I'll see everybody soon enough.

And we both know what that means. We eat the Mongolian Lamb and we don't talk about the late night vigil at Newspaper House and its implications. This now appears to be a conversation we are both quite determined not to have, so we eat and I think through my day. And if I described it to anyone, if I told them every part of it except the part going on in my head, it would look just right for a lazy summer day. Not a care in the world. But that's never been me, I suppose.

Later in my room I look at the poem I have begun. I have not begun a poem for a long time. I did not plan to begin one today. I read it through and when I read it I see it. It's very visual. It's a moment. Me trying to catch a moment. I have parts of it perhaps, but it was only ever just a glimpse. I can't glimpse it now, not quite. And the harder I try the more it's just words. Words trying to catch the shape they saw for a moment.

I'll look at it tomorrow.

I dream of exams but I wake to the sound of the sea and the sun of another bright day in my window.

I take seventy cents from the Big Pineapple ashtray in the kitchen and I leave the key in a shoe as I go.

There is no one out on the street yet, just the huge shadow of our house. It reaches across the road and onto the house opposite, the Keneallys'. It's still theirs, I think, but they aren't up here this summer. Chris and Emma are older than me, at uni now, and somewhere else these holidays, so their parents aren't at the coast. They've rented the house out all year and it's now lived in by at least six or seven people who are part of the way through the long process of stripping a Torana on the unmown lawn, draining thick old oil from some part of the engine into a pool that creeps onto the concrete driveway and forms an indelible stain, which they ignore.

Normally Chris and Emma would now be heading across the road to meet me, but not this year. This year there's just the long still grass and the burnt-orange shell of the Torana over there.

And next door the empty house of the Brunellos, which should at this moment be tipping out grandchildren to surf in large numbers. But the grandchildren now live in Adelaide and Mr Brunello looks tired when-ever he mows the large backyard that used to be our cricket pitch. He'd sit on his back deck while the dinner smells came down in the last of the light and he'd say, *Angelo Brunello, you call me AB, and I'm the captain till I'm ready to go.* He'd drink red wine and make changes in the field or chant the names of batsmen or bowlers and he'd set himself up as some omnipotent distant squareleg umpire. No one under the age of ten was ever stumped or run out.

This January the Brunellos have gone to visit their son and his family in Adelaide. They left before Christmas for a month or more and I've never seen their grass this long.

So there's just me left to surf this season's unimpres-sive waves. I walk around the corner of the house, past the washing line and across the sandy garden. The sun is low and coming off the water in a glare as I climb down through the she-oak trees and onto the beach. And there are a couple of cars in the Moffat Beach car park, probably boardriders, but I can't see anyone in the sea. An old man and woman walk slowly with their small dog. Up at the rocks someone is fishing.

The water is mine. I leave my towel and money and swim. I have a few half-decent rides and other people start arriving; a man with two young children, a girl and a boy. Perhaps they are at the beginning of these sum-mers, and just beginning to learn the rudiments of bodysurfing and cricket and the appropriate card games. They are slowly encouraged to head out from the shallows, and the man, their father maybe, starts to set them up for waves, to hold them up for the just-breaking waves to catch, their arms waving wildly. But

33

the timing's all wrong and they flail in the broken water as the wave runs on without them. So they swim back to the man and they stand on his hands and he throws them in the air and they come crashing to the water with that look of fear and excitement, and they struggle to the surface spluttering for breath.

Mr Keneally taught me how to bodysurf. Jim Keneally, Chris and Emma's father. The mechanics, the timing, the particular shape of the shoulders. He'd done it all his life, but he was a large man who came down the front of a wave like a truck and needed flippers to get started. I can remember I found the timing in a few days, and then distance. Past the others, past Jim Keneally kicking surreptitiously to drive his barrel of a body a little further in the unsupportive water. Green flippers tossing the water up behind him before he rolled over without speaking and turned to face the sea, and walked out for his next wave as I picked myself up where I'd hit the sand.

More people are arriving now, crowding the water. I go in to the beach, I take my towel, I walk to the showers.

I wash the salt away and rub the water from my skin. I head towards the newsagent with the towel around my shoulders and my coins in my hand.

And I see the girl.

I stop. I stop as though I've hit something. Because I wasn't expecting her and because she is right in my path.

She is in the car park with a car, a Moke. Just her and a Moke with the bonnet up and she is giving her engine the look of someone who doesn't know much about engines, but knows when to be unimpressed.

I'm not ready for this. It's early in the day. There are other things in my head. I'm on my way to the newsagent. She's right in my way. To pass I would have to walk round her. She's wearing a baggy faded T-shirt with her wet pony-tail sending a slow dribble of water down its back. And she reaches into the engine with slender honey-coloured arms, stands on her toes to lean forward.

I start to walk past, to change my course a little in a way that will allow me to walk past, but I don't. As I approach she looks only more attractive and I feel more tense. I should leave this moment to another day. And then review it and perhaps decide it's not a moment for me and is safer left unrealised. This is the library moment, the babe encounter, the moment of maximum fear, an instant when fantasies are smashed. And I have left my conversation-of-desirability in another place. I should keep walking. This is a mistake and I am about to make a dickhead of myself.

I keep walking, but only towards her.

Um, is there anything I can do? I say to her, in a voice not unlike that of a scared small boy, a voice that will not fill her with uncontrollable desire. A voice that she appears not to hear.

She keeps rummaging around deep among the unnamed oily parts of the engine. This would be a good time for me to walk away. Do you have a problem? I say, same voice as before. Meaning do you have a problem other than this pathetic nerd currently performing an unnoticed act of significant foolhardiness?

I think it's the clutch cable, she says, standing and turning to look at me.

And already I am entranced by her green eyes, her talking fine lips, the tidy lines of her unmade-up lips talking over her fine white teeth. Her compelling cat's eyes and her perfect skin and a small gold ring in her nose catching glints of the low sun. And I am saying, Oh, and nodding knowingly and vaguely hearing her saying *clutch cable* and realising I've never heard of that part of a car before and she obviously has so maybe this is a big mistake. And she's looking at me, interested in my assistance.

So, I begin to say, what are you going to do?

Well, I think it's just disconnected. It's a new one and my father's just put it in but I think it might have become disconnected.

Right.

So it needs to be reconnected.

Yeah.

If it's working.

Yeah. How would you reconnect it?

Tools. Do you have any tools? Screwdriver? Wrench?

Not with me, no.

Anywhere nearby?

I'm not sure. I live nearby, and there might be tools, but I don't really know much about engines.

So when you offered to do something, what did you have in mind?

I don't know. A push start maybe. But that probably wouldn't be much use, would it?

No.

Right.

So I'll have to call my father. You don't have any money you could lend me, do you, for the call?

No, not with me. I was just swimming. You can phone from my house if you like. It's not far. You can see it from here, the white house through the trees, I say, pointing. The one that backs onto the beach.

Okay.

We walk there, across the park where I quietly drop my seventy cents into the long grass. I try to lift my shoulders out of their normal slouch and try to cover most of myself with the towel. She walks beside me and I'm sure the people on the beach are watching us as though we're together, as though we haven't just met over a minor mechanical problem and I'm taking her to a phone.

We cross the beach and step up between the exposed roots of the she-oak trees into the garden.

Do you live here? she asks.

It's a holiday house. My parents own it. So I'm here every summer, and some other times. What about you?

I live here. Well not exactly here. Little Mountain, just inland. With my family.

Our feet make soft padded noises across the cool unlit grass and up the front steps, where I share with her the secret of the sandshoe. I half hope my mother will wake now, will come out of her room and find me with the girl I have brought home. But I also hope she will sleep deeply and not take this unlikely moment away.

I tell the girl that my mother is sleeping in, so she talks quietly on the phone. I shouldn't listen but I do because I want to hear every word she says. And all the time I'm thinking what do I do now? what do I do now? but I can't think of anything and this is all passing far too quickly.

My father will be a while, she whispers. *He's tied up. Something he can't leave.*

Oh, right.

So I guess I should get back to the car and wait for him there.

You can wait here if you want. You can probably see the car from the veranda. You might as well stay and have something to eat rather than just sitting down there.

She thinks about this and then says, *Okay, thanks*, with a small smile, but maybe just the smile you give in return for food. I don't know.

We've got bread and cereal and things, and tea and coffee. What would you like?

What kind of tea do you have?

What kind? Well, bags mainly, I think. Will that be okay?

Yeah. But what kind of tea is in the bags?

Oh, right.

At this point I realise I have been less than impressive

38

with the tea issue and I take her to the cupboard to show her the range available. Fortunately my mother is a bit of a tea fan and has teas to suit all tastes and occasions. The girl takes time with her decision, as though the choice is important, and she eventually picks something herbal and drinks it without milk or sugar. I do the same and it's pretty awful, but I think she thinks I do it all the time.

We sit on the veranda with our unsweet strange-tasting tea, eating toast with honey from the Caloundra markets and no margarine.

I know these people, she says, pointing to the honey jar. *It's good honey. Second best in the area.*

And already she makes this place into something different, just with the fragrant tea and second best honey that were here before her.

This is good bread, she says. *Who made it?*

Coles, I think. It's one of the breads they make there. It's from the one on the way into town, where you turn off to come here.

Really? My father makes our bread. Sometimes it's great. But this is good bread too.

So how long have you lived at the coast?

A couple of years. We've moved around a bit. It's good here though, I suppose. We used to be up north. It was okay there too.

But then you came down here?

Yeah. A couple of years ago.

We come here every summer. Every summer that I can remember. I live in Brisbane the rest of the time. Sometimes we come up during the year for weekends or a week maybe, but we're only here for a long time during summer.

Oh.

Do you surf here much?

No. I surf where the waves are, and they're not usually good here. They've been okay the last couple of days.

Okay, but not good. It hasn't been a good summer for waves, not anywhere around here.

No. Have you got a board?

No. I've got a ski, but I usually bodysurf.

She just smiles. This was not a good answer. Bodysurfing is not cool. Bodysurfing is not a reasonable thing to do, when seen from the perspective of a board-rider. Geeks rolling round in the shallows, thinking they have some association with the waves.

Do you want any more toast? I ask her, to divert attention away from being a bodysurfing geek.

Yeah. Thanks.

I go into the kitchen and while I'm waiting for the toast I try to work out what to say next. Try to work out what to say that will mean I see her again. The toast pops. She walks in smiling. She's killing me with this smiling.

She walks with a pantomime quietness so as not to wake my mother and she says in a loud whisper, *Still no father,* and shrugs as she takes the toast and covers it with honey. I make more for myself and we go outside.

So what do you do in Brisbane? she says. *School?*

Yeah. Well not any more.

I don't believe it. Here I am in the middle of fumbling my way through the enactment of a fantasy and it all gets back to that. The waiting. This is the moment when I should pinch myself and wake, find myself in bed with the light on and the loose sheets of the notes for my

40

poem crushed around me and the clock saying 3:00. This is when the dream gets worse and I look down and I'm not wearing any pants, not wearing anything at all, naked and blue as a smurf, crossing cartoon legs across tiny blue smurf genitalia.

But today this doesn't happen. She's expecting me to elaborate. Looking at me as though there's more.

You've left school? she says eventually. *Or finished?*

Yeah, just finished. Waiting. Waiting to see what I get.

Your offer?

Yeah.

When is that? Soon?

About sixteen days.

About sixteen days? She's smiling again.

Yes.

Sixteen days and counting.

I just happen to know the date.

You knew it was exactly sixteen days.

Okay, so I'm waiting.

What are you waiting for?

Arts/Law. Queensland Uni.

And what score did you get? One?

Two. A not very good two.

A not very good two. So where does that leave you? Close?

Yeah.

Sixteen days to go, hey?

Sixteen days.

What made you pick Arts/Law?

I don't know. What makes anyone pick anything? I don't know. I looked around. There were a lot of things I figured I'd hate. That wasn't one of them. I picked it.

41

It's only through everyone asking me what I've put that I've started to grow attached to it.

She laughs.

There's my father, she says. *Through the trees. That's his van just pulled in next to my car. I'd better run. He'll think I've been abducted or something. You know the way fathers are.*

She smiles and she goes. Down the steps and through the trees and off along the beach, leaving only the last corner of toast.

And I watch her go all the way to her car, before heading inside.

Inside where it is the same as always, still quiet and cool, my mother still sleeping.

10

The honey is out, and two plates, two chairs by the table through the open door. But the silence is back, the old silence that just minutes ago was talk. Now it's just me walking about on the seagrass matting, dry grass noises under bare feet, taking two plates to the sink and washing them, rinsing their crumbs away with cold water and wiping them. Old brown plates, old brown chip-edged plates, here all my life. I broke one when I was thirteen, washing up after dinner, dropped one and caught it but it smashed and I still have the scar, the faint white line of the scar on my left index finger.

Her voice is gone now, even if I try hard to keep it. Gone like a TV turned off.

I put the plates away, the knife away, the cups away, wipe the board, wipe the bench and the kitchen is clean.

I take another seventy cents from the Big Pineapple ashtray and I leave the key in the shoe as I go. And this reminds me, just as I drop the key, of Bill Murray in the movie *Groundhog Day*, but I couldn't be that lucky. First meeting after first meeting until I get it just right.

In the long grass I find the fifty from before, but not the twenty.

Her car has gone and there are other people in the car park now, and on the beach.

And I know nothing about her, still, really nothing. Not even her name. What does she do? What happens in her life? How do I know none of it? She drives a car, she lives nearby, she has green eyes and a small gold ring in her nose and a voice not quite from here. She makes me think of Angie Hart from Frente, the ring, the voice that only one person has, the compelling lightness.

Of course I went through a phase when I was sure there was nothing finer than Angie Hart. That's part of this now. Part of why the dream suspended at a distance was not shattered by the improbable meeting. She is still elusive, still desirable.

I'm not sure the Angie Hart phase ever ended. Other things happened, real people came along. Juliet maybe, if all that counts as real, but I still have the Frente poster on my wall. *That girl with the nose ring*, my mother said, trying to work it all out. I like the music, I told her, my head nodding to back up the tone of sincerity I was working hard to contrive. You should listen to the music. *But Kelly Street*, she said, *Accidentally Kelly Street, and that bit about it being a place where people would sometimes meet?* There's more to it than that, I told her, implying it was a generational thing, that she was of another age and could never understand. And doing that because I know she hates it. My mother who likes to be in touch with youth, needs to be in touch with youth and treats sick uni students, is blasé about condoms and STDs and all the other uni issues. My mother who is happy to tell anyone that she plays touch football, but never mentions it's in a veterans' competition. My mother who, I suspect, secretly extends her definition of youth a year with each birthday and who yearns for her son, caught in the trap of his own youth, to be interesting.

But this is hardly fair. If it was, she would have had her nose pierced to stop her losing touch, she might have experimented with grunge. But she didn't, and she will still argue with anybody that Fleetwood Mac's 'Rumours' is one of the Top Ten albums of all time.

So the girl reminds me, at least in some ways, of Angie Hart, but I don't know her name, I don't know how to find her, I don't know if she's forgotten me already. The socially disadvantaged nerd with the coat-hanger shoulders who lured her back to his house for toast and honey, who fought his way through a conversation as though each word was sticking to the roof of his mouth. Offering help he obviously couldn't give, offering tea he didn't understand, confessing to body-surfing, exposing himself as a tertiary entrance dickhead. All of this and moments of a strange intimacy, brought upon us by the need for quiet. Sometimes like two old people, nothing to say after all these years, scraping away at their breakfast toast. And all the time I was going crazy, trying to be calm but going crazy. Wanting her to want me, to stay, to take me with her, to touch me. Standing close to her as she whispered, *My father will be a while*, as though this gave us time. As though it defined a time that was ours. And then of course he came and she was gone, and I'm left with the day, the *Courier-Mail* that I'm carrying home, my late-sleeping mother, cricket maybe on TV.

My mother wakes, asks about the paper and I tell her the usual. I read my novel on the veranda, lying in the shade and looking at the page, blurring the words with a long gaze. Len waves from next door, makes the pool signal and we play.

I don't know what happens next, or if nothing has happened at all.

In the house I look for clues, but there is no sign that she was ever here.

11

In the afternoon I go to the mail box. There are no letters today. There is a medium-sized Vegemite jar containing honey. I open the lid and the honey smells of flowers, small sweet bush flowers.

There is a note. It says, *Thanks for breakfast. F.*

12

F.

Now she is F.

Fiona maybe? I try it out and it doesn't seem like her. But that doesn't mean anything. If I wrote a note and signed it A, would she work it out? I don't imagine so. I'll leave her at F for the moment.

I don't read my book, though I sit with it open in the hot windless shade on the veranda. I can see the Moffat Beach car park and through the still trees the beach, the glaring sand, people under umbrellas reading fat holiday novels.

Later I swim, but she's not there. It's back to what I'm used to, the waves and me. I walk round to Dicky Beach when I see she's not at Moffat, but I still don't see her so I swim.

F.

One encounter, honey, a note. Can I expect to see her again? Is this finished for her, complete with the gift of the honey? Did she meet her father and did he say to her, *Someone gave you breakfast? You'll have to pay them back. Why don't you drop over some small gift. Maybe some of that honey?* Did he tell her to write a note, just something short, because that would be polite. So now she will avoid Moffat, not just for better surf beaches.

This is all too plausible.

I look at the note. I stare again into its nineteen letters but not one of them tells me anything about her. There is nothing to tell me if she had more on her mind, more that she wanted to say. Nineteen neat pencil letters on a square of rough recycled paper, folded once. I could take a week to work on such a note and in the end send no more than nineteen letters. I see her going out into the trees for the wild honey, and finding it for me. And I am turning this into such an uncompromising fantasy I can almost hear the music as she dances through the trees in some diaphanous white gown, in slow motion like *Picnic at Hanging Rock.*

I should try to re-establish some attachment to reality and resume my life outside the F-note. Reality. Beach holiday. Me, my mother, swimming, books, her sleeping in, etcetera. One day like another, and that's not such a bad thing.

We eat pizza for dinner, my mother and I, and she says I'm quiet and I tell her it's part of relaxing. But I can't tell her about F. I can't say there's this girl. F, I think her name is, there's maybe more but I know her as F, and she had breakfast here today and she left me honey after, so maybe it was a good day. And I don't know what happens now, but I can think of a million and one possibilities. You know how it is. But she doesn't know how it is. She's far too naively optimistic for me to let her in on the matter of F. We'd both start getting our hopes up. I say nothing.

I sit with my book, I watch TV. My mother makes tea and talks about beach erosion and not really wanting to go back to work next week.

And later, in my room, while she's falling asleep reading in hers, I find the honey and the note again. I have them in a drawer and I want to check to see that they're both still there, that they do exist, and they do.

She didn't need to give me the honey, she really didn't.

I dip my finger in it and suck it, and I go to bed, my mouth full of curious sweet flowers.

13

I dream of nothing at all. I wake with scale on my teeth and the last picture of my non-dreaming night hanging like a clean white sheet. It's warm already, and later than usual.

I take my towel from the veranda rail and I go down to the beach. Her Moke is not in the car park near the shops, and I don't see her in the surf. Somewhere between here and the hinterland, maybe off some beach on this long coast, F is doing something this morning, but I don't know what, I don't know where. And I don't know how I might find her if I decided to look.

F.

F and her honey. Honey that maybe just repaid the favour of breakfast. Honey I should eat, a jar I should then throw out with the others. A jar that might then be recycled, might end up again in her hands, filled with her honey. To be sold somewhere, given to someone.

I swim and I watch the cars drive down the hump of Moffat Headland, down Queen of Colonies Parade, some parking in the car park, some driving on.

When I leave the water I realise I've forgotten the seventy cents for the paper. I could go home without the paper and stay. I could go home and have breakfast and not buy the paper today, but my mother would wonder why and ask me. *But you always buy the paper,* she would say. So I go home and take the money from its usual place and I walk back along the beach to the newsagent.

And I spend the day waiting, but I'm not entirely sure what for. Waiting for something to happen as though I am powerless to make anything happen.

My mother goes to Noosa for lunch with a friend, one of her uni friends who is also no longer married. They will take hours over the meal and wander up and down Hastings Street, window-shopping and stopping occasionally for coffee. My mother will be back with an armful of glamorous bags and a badly damaged credit card and she will deal with this by telling me how much Gina spent.

There's some of that chicken left for lunch, she says as she goes, *and some Coles salads.*

This would usually be a good time to play pool with Len, but he and Hazel are taking a bus-load of the oldies somewhere for the day. Len will make sure that wherever they are they'll manage a few beers with lunch and he'll have them all singing "Brown Slouch Hat" on the way back to the Home. And when he drops them off he'll say, *I think you'll find they'll sleep well tonight, Matron,* with a big wink, and the old diggers will stagger off the bus saying, *Good on ya Sarge,* because there were several times during the war when Len was a sergeant, though he never held the rank for long. *Busted for the stupidest things,* he will have told them long ago, just like he's told me. *I even lost a bloody stripe before El Alamein for eating a square of my chocolate ration early.* So they like to call him Sarge, even though he was more often a corporal at best.

Without Len there is no pool and no poetry, and the place is quiet because there is nothing going on but waiting. And it's driving me fairly close to crazy. I know she's out there.

14

By mid-afternoon I am still sitting on the back veranda with my book. Still sitting, more than half way through it now, but thinking about going down to the beach again. I hear feet on the front steps. A voice calls *Hello.* It's her, it really sounds like her.

F.

I stand up and drop the book and I say, Hello, back and I walk to the sliding door at the other end of the veranda.

Hi, she says, seeing me from the top of the steps and through the living room. She is smiling.

I reach for the screen door and, forgetting it needs to be handled gently, I de-rail it and it falls away from me and into the living room, hitting the nearby bean bag with a wheezy thump and sliding off onto the floor in front of me. I am left standing like a stereotypical silent-movie idiot, my hand still feeling for the long-gone door handle, the fallen door barring my way. She is at the front of my house and I am at the back of my house, wrecking the house that stands between us in order to get to her. She is of course laughing now. It would be a mistake for her to make any attempt to avoid laughing at an incident of such cruel comedy. But she makes no

54

attempt whatsoever, and she laughs a lot.

I pick up the door, fortunately without damaging anything else, and I lean it against the wall, trying to make it look as though I do this all the time.

Is it damaged, she asks me, *or does it just need a push start?*

It falls out a lot, I tell her. All the time. You wouldn't believe how easy it is to do that to that door. We should pay for someone to fix it properly.

I open the front screen door with great caution.

A lot of very sophisticated people have done that to that back door you know.

I'm sure they have. And I'm sure some of them went the same shade of red. Do you want a swim?

Yeah.

I just thought I'd drop round cause I thought I'd go for a swim and the surf's much better at Kings. I didn't know if you had a car so I thought I'd drop round and see if you wanted to go there. In case you were thinking of going for a swim.

Yeah. That'd be good. Let me just lock up what's left of the house.

I go round locking and shutting things and trying not to think about the door incident, trying to re-define it in a more positive way. There isn't one, but she's still here, waiting to take me to Kings Beach in her Moke.

We drive up Maltman Street and she apologises for the radio being old and only AM. There's country music coming through, filled with static, and she turns it off as though I might hold her responsible for the programming.

What does F stand for? I ask.

What does F stand for?

Yeah. F.

Lots of things I suppose. Why? Is this a car game, like I Spy or something?

Your name. Doesn't your name begin with F?

And there is a horrible fear running through me, telling me that I invented the honey, the note, and that this is where I do my cause irreparable damage. Just here near the lighthouse, on the crest of the highest hill around, an enormous view with nothing beginning with F, nothing that would let me change my mind and make it I Spy.

Oh, that's right. The honey. Did I just put F? I hope you liked the honey.

Yeah, the honey was really nice. Thanks. And F, the F on the note?

Sorry, that's just habit really. Leaving notes for my family when I go out. Of course, they know what comes after the F, so I don't need to put the rest.

She stops then, as though it is answered.

I don't have the rest, I tell her. I don't have the bit after the F. Okay, let's do this the obvious way, as though we've just met, and not over a clutch cable, or breakfast, or honey. My name is Alex.

And mine, she says, *mine starts with an F.*

That's all I'm getting? F?

It's a start. It's a good start. There are a lot of names that don't start with F.

And I have to guess now?

If you want to. Nobody's making you. F might be enough for you.

Maybe you're right. Maybe I should be grateful, I tell her. Here I was sitting around having just another holi-day at the coast, catching a few waves, fixing cars for friends, and all of a sudden I've got F. You're right. It would be greedy to ask for more. Fiona.

Fiona. And she says Fiona as though she is thinking about it very seriously. No.

Not Fiona.

No. Not even close.

Not even close? What's close to Fiona?

Nothing that matters to you, Alex.

Don't say that.

What?

My name. You tricked me. You shouldn't have my name. You should just have an A. An A would be tough.

F will be tough enough, Alex.

Fran. Anything like Fran. Frances.

She shakes her head.

Can I buy another letter?

I'll give you another letter. And to show you how generous I am, I'll not only give you a vowel, but I'll make it the second letter. O.

O. F, O. Fo.

And this has me thinking, the rest of the way to Kings. She parks the car.

Are you making this up? I ask her.

She laughs. *No.*

Is it, don't take this the wrong way, but is it a weird name?

A weird name. Don't take this the wrong way, but I bet you think a lot of names are weird names.

Fo. That's all I've got. Fo.

And the next day I see you I might give you another letter.

Okay. Okay. Is it a long name?

57

It's quite a long name.
And do I get a letter a day?
Maybe.
Okay. Okay Fo. I can be patient.
Then let's swim.

And with that she takes her T-shirt off, and she has a body that makes me realise I should have worn board shorts. So already I like her, she behaves as though she might like me, she plays consistently with an irresistible elusiveness, and now the body. The body in a blue and white striped one piece and I'm about to drop my shorts to my multi-coloured Christmas-present dick togs. The dreaded DTs that highlight every male contour. I sense this would not be a good point in our relationship to be carrying obvious signs of arousal in my togs. So I try to contemplate only the intellectual dilemma of her name, and I run quickly into the water, just in case.

So show me your stuff, she says, surfacing beside me after diving under a wave. *This bodysurfing you've been doing all your life.*

The waves aren't great, I tell her.

I know. That's why I didn't bring my board. Come on, impress me.

So we catch a few and of course she knows what she's doing, but she doesn't have a body like mine so she doesn't quite make the distance.

You're not bad for a city boy, she tells me.

And when she takes me home she says she'll stay for a drink and we sit on the veranda with mineral water and I wonder when my mother will turn up. I can't cope with the idea of having to introduce someone to my mother by using only part of their name, and fumbling my way through an explanation that sounds more like 'Wheel of Fortune'.

Fo. What kind of name does that begin? We talk and there are no clues.

There's no one here, she says.

No. My mother's gone to Noosa for the day.

There's just you and your mother then?

Yeah. Well, I have a father as well, but he isn't here. He's in Brisbane, with family number two. I usually spend a week or so up here with him each holiday, usually before Christmas, then a couple of weeks with my mother. Christmas Day is often the hand-over period, but that can be subject to negotiation.

Who does the negotiating?

Me. My Mother. We have custody of me.

I make her laugh with this, which is good. I don't want her thinking my family arrangements are a big deal.

We call the shots. But my father's pretty good about that sort of thing. He's not great about a lot of things, but that one he's fine with. He'll go along with what I want when it comes to what I do for summer. What about you?

What about me? Summer's pretty busy for me. It's a great time for making money out of tourists. Not that we're ever out to make a lot but if we have a good summer the rest of the year's much easier. We're more established down here now though, now that we've been here a couple of years.

So what do you do?

Well, there's the honey and other things like that. And things we make.

You make money out of honey and things you make? That's wild.

It's not a new idea.

What do you make?

A few things. My father's the main maker of things. He's a potter, I suppose, but he does a few things. My mother runs it all. My sisters and I go to school, or we have been going to school. I've finished now. We help out when we can.

So what are you going to do now that you've finished school?

Make things, I suppose. I haven't got any definite plans. Not yet. I'm pretty comfortable with all this, living here, catching a few waves when I can. I'm in no hurry to move on.

What about the future?

The future? Like Arts/Law Queensland Uni? I just have a funny feeling that's not my future. There are a lot of people who want all that stuff. I'm happy to leave it to them. And I think some of them are just doing it because people expect them to.

Yeah. Or because they're not so good at making things. I once made a cake tin at school and the first time my mother used it one of the ends came undone. I think she knew it was going to happen. I could just see by the way she looked at it when she was putting the mixture in. And pretty soon it was sitting on the bottom of the oven like a big overdone biscuit.

This is, of course, only one of many such stories of ineptitude, but she has already lived through the clutch cable fiasco and the screen door, so I decide not to bore her with any more examples.

She stays a while longer and we sit on the veranda with our legs hanging over the edge, leaning on the lower rail, drinking our mineral water. And she tells me

60

about her family and their several hectares of bush at Little Mountain, her younger twin sisters whose names both start with S, and her parents C and G.

I am beginning to wonder if she has somehow intruded upon my library fantasy, where alphabetically adjacent authors are instrumental in the babe encounter.

The breeze comes in, soft off the sea, and it pushes the waves of her hair around and she tucks them out of the way with her fingers, casually braiding the strands as she talks. She has fine fingers and hair all the colours of sand, white, ochre, ash. This I can see now I'm closer, and more of those green eyes. And I imagine the city taking all these colours away, and F wilting like an exotic plant taken to a cold climate and kept indoors, her hair turning to a limp brown, the emerald light in her eyes fading to a dull green-grey, her honey skin turning pasty. Maybe she needs this light, the space, the sea breeze.

She tells me she has work to do, things to make.

I'll see you soon, she says when she goes, and she gives me a smile that says she likes this game where she decides when soon is, and I don't even know her name.

15

My mother returns without bags.

You'd be proud of me, she says. *Apart from lunch and coffee I didn't spend a cent.*

What went wrong? I ask her. Noosa can't have run out of your size.

Well if it has I wouldn't know. That never became an issue. This was not a shopping day for Gina. Gina. And she throws her hands in the air, as though this is some joke at the expense of her very expressive friend. Man trouble, she says. *Man trouble. They're all bastards you know. You can't trust them.*

I say nothing. Gina has had man trouble before. Once she had such bad man trouble she even had her dog de-sexed. *I won't have balls in my house*, she told my mother, or so my mother's story goes. This is perhaps not the time to remind her.

My mother continues. *So whatever you decide to be, for God's sake don't be a man.*

You parents, I tell her, sometimes you have such unreasonable expectations of your children. What do you want me to be when I grow up?

Don't grow, she implores me. *Don't even grow into clothes.* Still waving those hands around in a way that turns everything she says into a ridiculous emphatic pronouncement. *Stay young and beautiful and unspoiled.*

Do you know how hard it is to get spoiled these days? Do you know how hard I've tried to get spoiled, but I've been brought up responsible. Once again I am nothing more than the victim of rigid parenting. But in the end that's all going to pay off and I imagine I'll grow up to be just like my father.

Don't make me angry.

Hey, I'm male. I'm likely to make you angry. It's the ball thing, remember? I take no responsibility for my chromosomes.

No responsibility. No responsibility. You learned that from a man, right? I didn't teach you that.

She makes a pot of tea and we drink it on the back veranda. She tells me about Gina and the man, the man Gina met through an agency who had written on his form *looking for a committed relationship.* He had written this down; he had not simply ticked a box. Gina had not felt good about going to an agency in the first place, and she had chosen to meet this man because she too was *looking for a committed relationship.*

So they had lunch a couple of times, my mother tells me, *because lunch is pretty safe and it gives you a chance to check someone out. But the third time they met he was all slime, and it became very clear that his view of the way these agencies work differed from Gina's. So that was that.*

I imagine it wasn't. I imagine my mother heard every grim detail, but I'm quite happy with this shortened version.

So we talked. We sat there with this great ocean

view, drinking coffee and talking about all of this, and there was no need to be in Noosa at all really. We didn't shop; she didn't want to shop. She's really not very happy. She wasn't happy before but she's worse now. I wish she could just work out that she doesn't need anything like that for her to be happy. But what can I do?

I am not expected to answer this, just to make an mmmm noise and go along with it.

So how was your afternoon?

Fine.

Of course, that's all I say. Fine, pause. And any opportunity for saying more slips by in an instant, so by the time I've gone Fine, pause, I can't say anything else or it might mean far too much.

Fine. I went for a swim.

What a change. Endless variety, these holidays provide for you, don't they?

I'm not complaining.

Particularly, I'm not complaining about how yesterday's sarcasm becomes today's irony so effortlessly. If I had to complain about anything at the moment it would be my mother's expectation that I go back to Brisbane with her at the end of the week. This bothers me all the rest of the afternoon.

We go to the Boits' around six-thirty. Len and Hazel have invited us over for a barbecue and I can already hear activity in the kitchen before we reach the door.

Come on in. Come on in, Len says, seeing us through the screen. *I'm just tossing the salad.*

He wipes his hands on the apron he is wearing to protect a lively Hawaiian shirt. He goes to the fridge to pour my mother a glass of cask wine and fetch me a beer.

How was Noosa, Tessa? he says, still facing the fridge and obscuring almost all of it with his large frame. He holds the glass in his left hand and turns the spigot with his right and the wine dribbles noisily, as though he is nonchalantly weeing into his veggie crisper. I try very hard to put this image from my mind, but it isn't helped when he gives the near-empty cask a bit of a shake to get the last of it out.

Fine, my mother with her safer side-on view tells him. *Like it always is, busy and very fond of itself. Didn't find anything I had to buy though.*

And your day, young Alex? How was it? He gives me a big wink as he turns. My mother notices.

Good. Good. It was good. I had a swim or two.

Of course I say this slowly and carefully, to give nothing away, but that only makes the wink more suspicious. My mother is looking at me now. She says nothing.

Surf's not great, I go on to say. It's okay, but it's not great. How was your bus trip?

They seemed to like it. One or two of the fellas might have had a beer too many at the Ettamogah Pub on the way back, but it didn't stop them singing.

The doorbell rings.

That'll be Clive and Alma. Could you get that, Haze. I'm knee deep in salad.

Clive and Alma inevitably ask me about school and I have to tell them I've finished and I don't know what I'm doing yet.

Be another couple of weeks, wouldn't it? Len says, still working the salad.

Yeah. Yeah, two weeks. Two weeks tonight actually. That's when we'll all be at Newspaper House buying the first of the *Courier-Mails.*

So how do you feel about it? Alma says. *I hope you're not letting it get you too worried.*

We're trying not to dwell on it too much, my mother says. *We can't do anything about it now. It's pretty tough all this waiting though. Isn't it, Alex?*

I'm getting used to it.

Then we briefly have the Arts/Law conversation and I give my standard uninterested explanation of tertiary entrance procedures and Alma and Clive give the standard response that things seemed a lot more straightforward in their day. *Of course, not a lot of people went to uni then. Most of us just left school and went to work. But it's different now, I suppose.*

I think Len can tell that this conversation is killing me and he says, *Let's go outside and get started on the barbecueing.*

We leave the others in the kitchen, and I can hear my mother being drawn into a conversation. The screen door slaps shut behind me.

We've got some of those gourmet sausages from the deli, Len tells me. *Thought we'd experiment.*

They cook with a smell of soy and honey mingling with the barbecue smoke and it's my job to turn them. Len splashes his beer over the steaks and it spits and dims the coals and rises in a cloud of musty steam. He deals with the steaks like a scientist, turning them as though there is only one right moment, as though the slightest hesitation or misjudgment would see them ruined. He has a reputation to uphold.

So, he says as though it's nothing, as though it's part of everything else, *how's your girlfriend?*

Girlfriend?

Friend of the young female persuasion. Girlfriend.

66

The one who was over yesterday morning. The one who drove away just after we got home this afternoon. That one. Not that I'm being nosey. Far be it from me to take an interest in other people's business, but Haze was just wondering. You're not planning to keep her a secret, are you?

No. No, not at all. Not that she's my girlfriend, necessarily.

Not necessarily?

I just met her.

Pretty poor timing isn't it? Meeting a girl and then going back to Brisbane. Unless she's from Brisbane.

No, she's from here.

I turn a few sausages. Len turns a few steaks.

I want to stay, I tell him. I don't know how long, but I want to stay up here a while. I don't have to go back to Brisbane. Not yet. My mother's going back to Brisbane though. It's a problem, maybe.

He seems as though he's thinking about this. *I'll have a word with her, if you want, your mother. I'll talk to her. If it'd help. Not about anything in particular of course, just a casual mention about you staying maybe. And how we'd keep an eye on you, that sort of thing. The sort of thing Tessa would want to hear. Would that be worth a go?*

Yeah, it might.

Does she know? About the girl?

No. I haven't said anything yet. I just met her. I don't know what to say to my mother yet. I like this girl. I think I really like her, and I just met her yesterday, so I don't want to go back to Brisbane yet. And that's maybe not an easy thing to explain to my mother. Remember that story, that one I wrote about the school play?

67

Remember how she handled that? I'm not ready for that yet.

He laughs.

I reckon you're about to charcoal a few snags, mate, he says, looking down at the sausages suffering on the barbecue plate in front of me. *We should be heading in.*

I reserve the darker, more damaged ones for myself and tell Alma and Clive I like them that way. My unexpected ally goes to work while my mother is helping herself to seconds of the salad.

You know, Tessa, Len says as though the idea has just come to him, *if young Alex wanted to stay up here a bit longer when you go back to Brisbane, Haze and I'd be happy to keep an eye on him. Wouldn't we, Haze?*

Of course, love, Haze agrees. *Happy to.*

My mother looks at me. She says nothing. I don't know if she's just looking for a comment or for signs of a conspiracy.

That might be good, I say, looking right back at her. There's no real hurry for me to get back, is there?

No. No, I don't think there's a hurry for any particular reason. I thought you were keen to catch up with your friends though.

Well, I will, soon. I won't be up here for ever. I'd want to be back before the offers come out anyway.

So how would you get back to Brisbane?

With you if you came back the weekend after next. Or the bus if you didn't, I suppose.

The bus. You've never been keen to catch the bus before.

I'm not keen now. It's an option. I haven't even really thought about all this yet, the idea of staying. Len just mentioned it. It just sounds like something to think about.

Sure, we can think about it.

When we're at home later I think about it a lot. I lie on my back in the dark looking up at the barely-visible pattern on the underside of the top-bunk mattress, and I think about it a lot.

16

Once, a few years ago, at school dancing classes I asked a girl for her phone number and she gave it to me. She wrote it on my hand because neither of us had anticipated this moment and we could find a pen but no paper. My friends were impressed and a couple of people at school even came up to have a look at my hand, which I took care not to wash long after I had copied the number onto paper.

I called her from a public phone on the way home from cricket practice one afternoon.

She said, *I'll just check with my mother.* After the longest pause I've ever known I heard her pick up the phone again and she told me, *My mother says I'm not ready to go out.*

Okay, I said, quite unprepared for this outcome. Some other time then maybe. And she said, *Yeah, well, 'bye then.*

So the next day I told my friends, and they all thought it an unfortunate but quite legitimate outcome. Just one of those things. Mothers.

I must have missed her emerging readiness by a matter of days, for it was no more than two weeks later that I went to the movies with the same friends to see

The Big Steal and she sat a couple of rows in front with some guy with shoulders who took several opportunities to send his tongue well past her tonsils. My friends thought it was a great movie. I thought so too, but not until the second time I watched it on video over a year later, when I decided I should forget the silhouettes that had writhed in front of me and instead try to believe the film's suggestion that sometimes the none-too-cool guy gets lucky indeed. That day in the dark at Hoyt's this had seemed a particularly transparent lie.

The length of the pause should have warned me even though my friends said that all pauses seem longer than they actually are when you're waiting for something like that, and besides, it probably meant she had had a fight with her mother because she wanted to go out with me. And I had liked that idea the whole two weeks, and I had thought we would meet at a school dance some time soon anyway. My friends told me this was likely.

But instead all that is likely is that she went to her mother and said, *What do I say to this guy?* and her mother said, *You could tell him I think you're not ready to go out with just one person yet, something like that.*

This was not a good thing to happen to someone who was already not great at taking the initiative. I don't think I've improved much since.

I think I just got lucky with F and her need to make a phone call. How is this so easy for her?

The morning passes. I swim and buy the paper. Gina calls. I hear my mother saying, *No, no, not at all. I think it's important to talk about these things.* Then a pause while Gina says something. *Of course you feel you're on your own sometimes but we can always talk. We can shop any time. Think of the money I saved.* Pause. *No, I was only joking. It was only a joke.* I go out onto the veranda to read my book.

Len takes me to the Powerboat Club for lunch and I watch the first hour or so of the cricket on the big screen. He joined the club years ago, when it was starting and life memberships were cheap, but it's different now, with the poker machines. Every month there's a flyer in the mailbox promoting upcoming visiting acts and regular events. Tomorrow, the Col Noble duo and soon Greg Doolan for Morning Melodies. Tuesday: Oriental Cuisine Night (Bookings essential). Monday: Bingo (Free Cuppa and Biscuit). Sunday: Sunday Madness.

Len's a lunch-time regular and a big fan of the fisherman's basket. On some days when there's cricket on I go with him to sit in the airconditioning and watch the game while he circulates, telling a few yarns, buying beers at the bar, blowing a few dollars worth of twenty-cent pieces over at the machines and then coming back to me for periodic updates. Today Australia loses two wickets early and scores slowly.

I swim again at the end of our innings and then I finish my book. Maybe I won't see her today. I play Frente's 'Lonely' EP repeatedly and when my mother asks if I'm trying to tell her something I put the headphones on and keep playing. This way it's even better, as though the voice is in my head. I think I bought the EP after seeing the filmclip for 'Bizarre Love Triangle', Angie Hart with straight short black hair and crimson lips, her pale face and sad-sweet voice. And in this incarnation she doesn't look much like F, at least not with the hair, but I can still find similarities, still hear

72

what I'm listening for.

Just as I fall asleep I think I hear my name called, but when I turn off the music there's only the sound of the sea, waves working their way up the beach again, and the fan turning and clicking on the other side of the room. I open the sliding door as quietly as I can and I walk onto the veranda. It's cooler out here, and far away there's a dog barking, maybe at the bright three-quarter moon.

After this it's harder to sleep. I didn't see her today, and usually I would assume the worst. But I don't with her. What I'm assuming is that I'll see her again, that she will choose to come to see me again.

That's not like me.

FROM THE FILMCLIP

These pictures are played
Again and again
In sometimes orange light
Sometimes blue

Warm then cool
Mouth red as paint
Calling a dance
Looking like slow
Slow motion

All like some magic
Some dream
Closing like cloud

And even in rain
Your eyes are not cold

17

On the beach in the morning is a word or, at least, four letters. F O R T, large capitals written in the untouched sand left by the receding tide.

She calls to me from the trees. *Any ideas?*

Fort? You're telling me Fort now?

That's right.

Fort. Like a military installation. Fort.

You can say it as many times as you like but it's not my name until you say some more.

Fort.

Consider yourself lucky. I gave you two letters. I meant to come down and give you the R yesterday but I got stung by bees in the afternoon. Just on the right hand so I didn't think I should drive. So I stayed home.

She opens her right hand to show me the lumps of stings at the base of the index finger and near the wrist.

Are they still sore?

Yeah. Not much though. They'll be better after a swim.

So where are we swimming?

Kings? There'd be better stuff at Kings.

Okay.

So what did you do yesterday? she says when we're on the road.

Not much.

Not much?

No. It will never be recalled as a day of great achievements. Just another one of those holiday days.

I don't think I have them. What are they like?

You hang around, swim, read. If there's cricket on TV your day has meaning. Otherwise you just hang round. Every few years something different happens, something you don't expect at all, something totally out of control. For example, your neighbour takes you to the Powerboat Club and instead of ordering the burger like you always do, you order the fisherman's basket, just like him. And he spends the rest of the day wondering why, looking at you like something's going on. I didn't do that yesterday though, I just ordered the burger. My life's crazy enough already, and besides he knows there's something going on.

He knows there's something going on?

Oh, yes. He's seen someone unfamiliar coming and going.

And has he worked out what's going on?

I don't know. He might have made assumptions, but I'm not in a position to speculate on their accuracy. Not that I'm one for speculating.

She laughs and she takes a corner. I like the way she drives. She seems very calm, at ease with the process. I notice this since I'm still learning and I am not calm when I drive. Each pedal, each switch, every part of the car is my enemy and hides when I need it. F drives as though each part is an extension of her, as though she and they have a comfortable association. I think her cool would intimidate me if she wanted it to. But she makes things cool without meaning to and

76

carries cool around with her. She wears clothes I could not normally forgive and she makes them cool, surf-hippy influences ending up somewhere near grunge, but not quite, not that aware, not that influenced. A shapeless old shirt and no shoes, old khaki shorts. The waves of her hair held back by elastic. All of it looser than I'll ever be, more recklessly at ease. Like this old car, open-topped and unsophisticated, kicking out of the pot holes, shaking up and down the hills, bouncing through this summer without a care. Without any idea that other cars might do it differently, with suspension and climate control and a radio with an FM option.

In this car you have to smell the summer, feel the sun on your skin, feel the wind slipping past you.

I want to ask her why all this is happening. Why she keeps coming, how long she will keep coming. This is great, but I want to understand it. And I want to know what to do next.

We swim and all I can say is, So what are you doing this afternoon?

Working, I suppose. Doing bee-keeper things, and other stuff.

What are bee-keeper things?

There are many secrets that can only be handed from bee-keeper to bee-keeper. I'm not sure a potential Arts-Law student should know them.

But what if I wanted to keep bees some time? What would I have to know?

It's not that easy. You'd have to start at the bottom, and the secrets come one by one, and only when the bee-keeper's ready to tell.

So tell me about the bottom.

The bottom. And she thinks. *The bottom is probably the jars.*

So what do I do with jars?

Three things. Scrounge them, clean them, fill them. That's all you need to know, other than labelling, but that's separate. More advanced.

I think I could do the jars now. I think I already have several of the skills required.

Yeah? So you want to do some jars?

Sure.

Okay. This afternoon, unless you're too busy holidaying. You could do jars while I do the really challenging bee-keeper things.

Okay.

Good. So I'll pick you up at two or so.

Good.

I realise then that I will have to tell my mother this. I will have to say something to her if I am planning to be away for the afternoon. This would be a good time to tell her, I decide. I just have to tell her not to get too excited about it when I do.

That would be a start.

18

Have you got any plans for this afternoon? I say to my mother.

No. Why?

I'm thinking of going out, that's all.

Out?

Yeah.

Doing anything in particular?

Yeah, helping someone with bees actually.

She laughs. *That's very funny. Obscure but funny. What are you really doing, or is it some secret?*

Helping someone with bees. Washing jars for the honey. They have to put the honey in jars to sell it.

When you've washed them?

Yes. That's right.

My mother is finding this highly amusing, and the only thing that in any way tempers her amusement is the thought that her son might have gone mad.

Could you explain that in a way I could understand? I see you sitting round, being a little tense, doing some reading, watching some cricket, swimming, all things that I understand, and suddenly you have a plan to go somewhere and help someone with bees. Who? And how do you know them so well that you want to go round there and wash jars?

Okay. First let me just say that it's fine. That it's nothing to be concerned about. It's just fine. I'll be fine. And it's no big deal. Okay?

Okay.

I happen to have met someone in the last few days who keeps a few bees. I thought I might as well do something useful, so I thought I'd go round and help her.

Help her. So this is some frail old bee-keeping woman and you're performing a good deed by going round there and helping?

Well, no. I have to be honest, no. She is not a frail old woman.

So tell me more.

She's closer to my age, and it's probably a big job, keeping bees.

Forget the bees. You've met a girl?

Well, yeah. And she's got bees.

Tell me about her. And I don't mean tell me about her bees.

I don't really know anything about her bees.

She gives me that look, that look that says she knows she's onto something and that I won't find myself anywhere near a bee until I tell her quite a bit more.

Okay. She's just a girl. I met her on the beach a couple of days ago. No big deal.

She lifts her eyebrows, a sign that I am to elaborate, a sign that she suspects I have given her only a dull subset of the story.

She lives near here, Little Mountain, with her family. They make things. That's just about all I know.

So exactly how did you meet her?

She had a problem with her car. I offered to help.

80

You can help people with car problems?

No.

It's a bold sort of offer then, isn't it?

It was all I had. There she was with her bonnet up. I had to do something.

So what did you do?

I brought her here to use the phone.

I can feel a nervous smile starting to take control of the corners of my mouth.

Really? That's very clever.

I gave her breakfast.

Breakfast? She ate a meal here days ago? Why are you smiling? So I begin to grin almost uncontrollably, one of those tight unmanageable desperate grins that is only muscular and recalls no happiness at all. *What did you do? What's that smile for? What have you been doing in this house while I've been asleep?*

Don't get excited, I tell her, trying to restore calm.

You haven't …

I haven't done anything. Okay? I have done nothing that would interest you. I have done nothing that would be worth telling people. We've gone to Kings Beach a couple of times because of the better surf, but that's all. Now, I think you're a bit too interested at the moment, and I think we're going to have to get you a cup of tea and calm you down, and we won't talk any more about this now.

She laughs at me treating her like the mad person.

All right, all right. Not another word.

Good.

What's her name?

We're not talking any more about this, remember?

Her name, just her name.

Okay, this is what we'll do. I'll give you the first letter of her name and if you behave appropriately, there'll be more later. And that includes being out when she arrives to pick me up.

In her car. I can't believe I notice so little. Here I am thinking you're sitting around doing almost nothing, and all the time you're involved with a girl with a car.

Look, it's not much of a car, I only met her a few days ago and I am not involved. Okay? Not involved. Helping her with issues concerning bee-keeping this afternoon. That's all. So will you be out when she comes to pick me up at two?

If it's what you want.

It's definitely what I want. What I would like is for you to go out and be out for quite a while. That is what I would like most.

All right. If it's what you really want.

I nod.

Why do you want to hide her from me?

That's not quite it. What I want to do is to hide you from her.

That doesn't sound like a very nice thing to say to your mother.

Just think about it. Look at it from my perspective.

What do you mean?

Does the name Juliet mean anything to you?

That was a beautiful story. A wonderful, sensitive story. I had to show people.

Exactly. There'll be no more of that. Okay?

Okay. It's okay if I get the first letter of her name.

F.

F. Fiona?

Not even close.

19

Are you sure you really have a mother? she says when she arrives.

I'm sure enough. She just happens not to be here this afternoon. She's probably shopping.

We drive out along Sugarbag Road to Little Mountain, past the cemetery and the high school and over the Nicklin Way, through bush and past the new developments.

My family'll be home, she tells me. *Some of them at least.*

We turn down a smaller road and through a gateway onto a path that looks as though it has been cut out of the bush. The Moke bucks around, but F makes little concession to the unmade road and I try to be subtle about gripping onto the sides of the seat. We pull up in a cleared area in front of a rambling wooden house.

A girl appears in the doorway. She is wearing a dress that looks tie-dyed and she has F's hair.

Hi, Skye. Come and meet my friend Alex.

Hi, Alex, she says, with a coy smile. *I've got a problem with my car.*

Skye, F says sternly.

What have you told her?

Nothing.

Nothing? Nothing? Am I dressed like a mechanic?

Skye is laughing. *He's better looking than you told us, Big. We thought he'd be pretty ugly, the way you described him.* And she runs off down the hall laughing and shouting, *Big's brought the boy home, Storm. Come and see.*

Did I tell you about my sisters? F says. *No self-control, none at all. I think you should know that.*

Thank you. Earlier might have been better, but thank you.

She was kidding with all of that. I might have mentioned the car, but she was kidding with the rest.

I bet she was. What did she call you?

Big.

Big? Why Big? I've got to be honest. You're a very reasonable size but you aren't big.

I am to her. It's short for Big Sister. When Skye and Storm were young they found it hard to say the F name, so they called me Big. You know the way families are. Someone does something like that and it sticks. They all call me that now, my whole family.

They never call you the F name?

Never.

So the whole time I'm here today no one is going to come up to you and call you by your name.

It's very unlikely.

I came here and I was sure someone would call you by your name.

I don't think they will. I'd quite like you to call me by my name. Almost nobody does, so I'd like that.

So are you going to tell me what it is?

Yes. She pauses, as though she's trying to remember

84

it. *Come and meet my dad.*

She leads me through the house to the kitchen and then down another corridor where she opens a door. In the centre of the room is a potter's wheel and next to it, working the day, stands a man with crazed feral hair and a wild beard with clay wiped through it. He appears to be wearing only a grubby vest.

He turns to face us and he is wearing only a grubby vest, and his turn swings his dick perilously close to the wheel. I open my mouth to say something, but I just can't.

Hi, he says with a very normal human smile. *You're … um.* Clicking spludgy fingers together and making no sound, cracking the drying clay on his brow with the furrows of thought.

Alex, F says.

Alex, he says, as though agreeing. *Nice to meet you, Alex.*

He stands there saying normal things and looking like a very cheery near-nude maniac with dirt mittens. A shiny, wet, unfinished pot wobbles around the middle of the wheel.

You too, I say. I hope not too slowly.

Cliff.

Cliff.

I think I'm nodding. I think I'm nodding in a ponderous mesmerised way and my mouth is probably open. So what do I say now? Nice pot? Do a lot of this do you? That's an enormous penis you've got there, Cliff? *Well thank you, Alex?* So I just stand there nodding, hoping the slow-swinging fleshy pendulum will not come to harm.

Oh, yeah, mate. I'm just airing a bit of a rash, he

85

says, as though it's an explanation. *Potter's itch, you know.*

F laughs and shakes her head. *Dad, you say that to everyone. Don't listen to him, Alex. This is what he always wears when he's potting.*

Even in winter?

Well, no, maybe not in winter. But potter's itch is just a joke for visiting yuppies. Don't say it to Alex, Dad.

Not a day for jokes, hey Big?

Not for yours, Cliffie.

Sorry. Sorry Alex. I think this must be one of those first impression things, and obviously Big wants me to create a good one. How am I going?

Great. I'd be lying if I said you weren't creating quite an impression.

Dad, I think he's hating you. He's got this sense of humour and I think he's hating you and that's the closest he can go to saying it. And I think it was the potter's itch thing. You treated him like yuppie scum and he knows it. I think he liked you till then.

That's not true, is it Alex? You didn't take it personally, did you?

No. No, not at all.

He likes me Big. I can tell. I like him, he likes me. It's one of those things, mutual. Pull up a seat, mate.

It is a room entirely without seats, so I take this to be a symbolic gesture.

You're meant to sit on that box now, Alex, F says, pointing. *Then he talks to you.*

I sit on the box, and I assume that the clay will wash out of my shorts.

So what about this place, eh? Cliff says, his eyes on his pot again as he works it back into shape.

It's great, I tell him. Great.

Yeah, but what about all the development going on? What about that?

Oh, that, yeah. Well, to be honest I could probably do without it.

Good on you, mate. There's only one thing worse than developers and that's people who think they're hippies. What do you reckon, mate?

What?

This strikes me as dangerous ground indeed.

People who think they're hippies. Live in the bloody hinterland and pretend they're dropping out. There's not one of them wouldn't shrivel up and die without town water. To them an alternative lifestyle means another way of making money. Maleny, Montville, all that. They're not hippies, they're wankers. What do you say, mate?

Well some of them seem a bit sus. Like they're only in it for the tourist dollar.

Exactly. Exactly. He's good this boy, Big. He's got a clue. A lot of people don't, you know.

Yeah Dad, I know. Is he boring you, Alex?

No, not at all. This is fine, really good.

Are you going to help me with the jars then?

Sure.

Perhaps I jump to my feet too quickly but Cliff still seems to like me when I leave the room. In the corridor F looks at me and laughs.

You're very funny, Alex, she says.

We go to another room where Skye is working at a table.

The bottle washer, she says, and smiles, then shakes her head knowingly. *My big sister, always bringing home boys and making them wash bottles for her.*

I'm sorry, F says to me. *You don't know Skye well enough to know that she lies all the time.*

Skye laughs. *All the time*, she says.

She has a sheet of labels which have been stamped with a black ink logo saying Big Buzz Honey, and her job seems to be to fill in two yellow stripes on the back of each bee. Mine is to deal with the sink full of jars soaking in the corner, to peel off their labels and clean them. I can't help thinking I would be unlikely to do this for my mother. F leaves to attend to bee-keeper things outside. Skye watches her go and then turns to me.

Big likes you, you know.

Aren't you the one who lies all the time?

Not all the time. That was a lie.

So what's her name? Big, what's her real name?

You'd be pretty stupid if you don't know that, she says. *Pretty stupid if you'd come to someone's house and wash things for them if you didn't even know their name.*

Yeah. Right. She laughs.

I keep washing, flicking the labels into another sink and washing.

20

That was a big help, F says as we drive home. *That's a pretty dull job and I was glad I didn't have to do it.*

That's fine. It was interesting meeting Skye and your father.

It's all right. You don't have to be polite.

They were interesting. They really were. Trust me.

Really? She shakes her head.

My mother's car is in the driveway when we arrive.

So she does exist.

I think you should know she's not quite like your family.

My mother is waiting, trying not to look like a spider in a web, but failing.

Hello, she says with significant enthusiasm, sizing F up from head to toe quite unashamedly. *I'm Alex's mother.*

Hello, I'm his friend, F says and smiles.

I'm Tessa.

And I'm Fortuna.

They both look at me, each glancing at me sideways but trying to appear to pay attention to the other.

Fortuna, my mother says. *That's a lovely name. Certainly not common though. It's not the sort of name you could ever guess.*

89

People tend not to.

They are both looking at me now, quite openly, as though each shares with me a deeply ironic joke that excludes the other. I can feel the smile freezing on my face.

Will you stay for a drink? my mother asks her. *A cup of tea maybe?*

Thank you. I'll just have the one I had last time, Alex, if that's all right.

This is becoming an afternoon of silly staring and my mother contributes once again, this time a withering knowing look referring to the breakfast I kept from her for days. We sit on the veranda with our tea.

So, my mother says, staring at the nose ring, *do you like Frente?*

Yeah. Yeah I don't mind some of their stuff.

Alex is a bit of a fan, aren't you Alex? He's been playing that CD, which one is it?

Lonely.

He'll wear it out if he plays it any more.

CDs don't wear out, Mum.

Silly me. Trapped in the age of vinyl.

So my mother decides to make this a fairly painful experience. She can't help herself. But Fortuna seems not to mind. She laughs at my mother's jokes at my expense, and tells me, *Your mother's really interesting*, when she goes. Of course, in the context of this afternoon that could mean anything. She gives me her phone number and she says she'll be busy most of the day tomorrow, but I can call if I want to. Then she gives me a look that tells me I should want to.

When I'm back upstairs my mother has the good sense to apologise to me about the Frente remark, but she negates the apology most of the evening by repeatedly making observations about nose rings. *Why would you have a nose ring? Why? How does she blow her nose? What's it like when she has a cold? What if it got caught on something?* Etcetera, etcetera, and all of this with her face in various masks of discomfort, until I tell her she's being very dull.

When I go to bed I play the CD again, and I listen to the name, the way she said it the first time, like a secret. Fortuna. It holds its own music; it's the sort of name she should have.

21

So this is why you want to stay up here? my mother says as she packs. *Fortuna? She's why you don't want to come back to Brisbane with me?* She throws dirty clothes into a garbage bag and she breathes heavily. *What are you going to do? Have you thought about it, all of it? Here by yourself. You would be here by your-self, wouldn't you? I mean, she's not going to move in, is she?*

No. I'll stay here; she might visit. Len'll be next door if I have any problems.

And I'll be back next weekend.

So it's less than a week. I'll be fine.

And you won't do anything, will you? I mean, you'll be sensible?

I'll be as dull as I always am. Give me a break. It's not like this was never going to happen. It's like schoolies' week, when we all went to the Gold Coast, and I survived that okay.

I suppose so. She goes on packing, putting away a hair brush, face cream. *What will I tell your grandpar-ents at lunch tomorrow?*

I can guess what you'll tell them. That I've met a girl and that's why I'm staying up here. That you think the girl is weird, mainly on account of the fact that she has a ring in her nose. But then, to avoid panicking them you'll have to say that she seems very nice really.

That sounds likely.

My mother leaves for Brisbane after lunch.

I call Fortuna, and it's strange hearing her voice on the phone, but it's good too.

Tessa's pretty cool, she says. *It's kind of nice that she likes Frente. I liked that. What made her say it, do you think? Just the fact that you'd been playing the CD?*

Probably.

We talk, even though there's nothing to talk about. I really like her voice and I don't want her to put down the phone. She tells me her father liked me a lot, and maybe Skye did too, from the unkind things she's been saying. She laughs, and won't tell me more. I ask if I'll see her later and she says *maybe*, and then she says *I hope so.*

I watch the cricket. I lie low in a bean bag in front of the small TV and I watch the screen between my knees. It's our innings and we're chasing a reasonable total.

Len comes over with a couple of cold beers. I move the bean bag round and he pulls up a chair nearby and sits forward on it, peering at the TV through the lower lenses of his bifocals.

Shame the West Indies aren't out here, he says. *I'd love to see Lara. He's good, isn't he?*

Yeah, he's really good.

I saw Bradman bat a couple of times, and it's not a comparison you like to make but ... He shakes his head. I am aware of the enormity of the comparison. *Sure his five-oh-one was against pretty ordinary opposition, but it's still bloody five-oh-one, isn't it? The highest test score and the highest first-class score within weeks of each other and by the same bloke. Who would have thought that'd ever happen?*

Yeah. I honestly didn't think either of them would ever go. I just didn't think there were enough overs in the day any more.

So we sit sipping our beers and solemnly theorising about the great game. This is one of life's significant pleasures that eludes my mother entirely. Once I won a voucher in a literary competition and amazed and appalled her by swapping it for a book of complete test cricket statistics. Every match, every innings, every individual score over forty and every haul of four wickets or more, since tests began in 1877. Batting and bowling averages and aggregates, by country and alphabetised, any individual or career record that could be conceived, usually with the top ten performances all listed.

But why would you want that? my mother said.

And the question cannot be answered. Anyone who asks it can never understand. I showed the book to Len and he looked up Spofforth's incredible performance on a sticky wicket in the 1880s, he looked up Bradman's 334 and he looked up the last test he had seen at the Gabba before the war.

And just how good was bloody Victor Trumper? he said, and he looked that up too.

He didn't ask me why anyone would want the book, and from then on I was expected to bring it to the coast with me each summer, as there were frequently issues one or other of us felt needed checking.

When he's finished his beer, he tells me there are a few things he should be doing in the garden. He invites me over for dinner later, another barbecue. Next door it is the season of salads and burnt sausages.

Unless you've got plans, he says.

No, no plans at all.

In fact I had not even thought of dinner. I suppose I would have worked this out at some time, and ended up walking down the road for a burger or fish and chips. It makes me wonder what else I should be planning, now that I'm here by myself.

You could invite your friend, he says, *if you like.*

So after he's left I call her again. She says she'll come.

22

At the barbecue I think I'm watching her all the time. I think I should be saying more, listening more, being more interesting, but I think I'm watching her.

Len easily fills in the spaces with talk, and even when he asks Fortuna something about herself, it often ends up with him talking again. He asks her how long she's lived around here, and then he tells her about the past, what it used to be like here years ago, when he was young and coming up here with a tent. She hasn't heard these stories before, and it seems to surprise her that it could have been so different here, so recently.

Makes you wonder what's going to happen next, she says. *What it'll be like in ten or twenty years time.*

Up at our house there is no movement, no sound. The lights are on in the living room and on the front veranda so I can make my way home, but the house is empty. I drink beer and we turn Len's latest selection of gourmet sausages on the barbecue. *Philippine style,* he says as they're cooking, *but I'm buggered if I know what that means.*

We sit eating and Fortuna tells Len and Hazel about her work for the markets tomorrow, the honey, the twins rolling beeswax into candles, Cliff firing coffee mugs in half dozens and making wooden stands with pegs to hang them on.

And I'm doing this thing, she says, with quite an intense expression as though in her mind she's doing it right now, *this thing with old stockings and grass seed, where I put some grass seed in the stocking and then stuff it with dried grass and make it into the shape of a head and I put a face on it and sell it. Then people water it and the grass sprouts as hair.* She laughs. *It's very popular. The most popular one is Merv Hughes, but I don't know why.*

He's a popular man, Len says.

Yeah, but I don't know why people would want to grow grass out of his head. What I want to do is a series of people whose hair already grows straight up and sell them as a boxed set. You know, Yahoo Serious, Kramer from Seinfeld, that boxing promoter, Don King. And she's nodding while she says all this, nodding quite earnestly. *Einstein maybe. People like that.*

We all nod too and make mmmm noises and try not to look at each other. I briefly wonder what the hell I'm doing hanging round at the coast to be with a girl who seems to think growing grass out of old stockings holds the key to her future.

She laughs. *I'm kidding*, she says. *That was a joke. You didn't think I was really going to do it, did you?*

You had me going, Len says. *All the way. Right from the Merv bit on.* And he laughs.

The Merv bit's true, she says, looking a little uncomfortable. *I make Merv heads. People buy Merv heads. I don't know what for, but people buy them. Birthday presents for people they don't like maybe. You can make five bucks for a reasonable size Merv head, ten if you sell it with a base.*

97

A base?

Yeah, a jam jar painted like a one day cricket outfit. My mother does those, I just do the heads. Seriously. You'd be surprised how many of them I sell.

Five bucks sounds like a bargain for a Merv head, Len says.

We go inside, into the pool room, and Len suggests a game of doubles.

I've never really played before, Fortuna says.

So you'll be on my team, Len tells her. *We'll be right.*

He rolls a few balls onto the table, hands her a cue and takes one for himself. He says it's a matter of simple geometry.

There's simple geometry? she says. *I should have concentrated more when we did those sines and cosines and things.*

The balls fly around crazily when she starts hitting them, but soon, with a few hints from Len about where to strike the cue ball and how to aim, she's crouched down over the table staring down the cue with one eye, taking on the pose of the master.

I can do this, she says. *Let's play.*

We rack the balls and I break. I watch Fortuna circling the table, studying the possibilities, playing and not quite putting the twelve-ball away into the middle pocket.

You've got a good eye, Len says. *Bloody good eye. Watch her, young Alex.*

A quite unnecessary remark, of course. I'm watching her already. Watching her move around the table as sleek as a cat, tilt herself into position to play. Watching her fingers around the cue, the bridge of her left hand, her left thumb turned up with the cue running next to it, the muscles of her forearm working under her tanned skin, her hair gripped in a scrunchie behind her head, loose strands falling across her neck like soft uncoiling springs.

I want to do more than play pool with her. Right now it's hard to stand here and just play pool, even when she's playing and enjoying it, having this uncomplicated good time, and close enough for me to touch.

It's my shot and I'm not playing well. My hand shudders just as I play and I miss an easy one that would put us ahead. It's up to Hazel to keep us in the game.

This is it, love, she says, and straightens her glasses.

She sinks the three but misses the five and sets Fortuna up for another shot at the twelve. This time it goes.

Nice one, partner, Len says.

When it's my turn again I breathe deeply, concentrate, blow it again. My game is only deteriorating.

Not your night, is it mate? Len says and turns to Fortuna. *He usually cleans up. Makes me look like a joke most days. Don't you mate?*

Not that I've noticed. But I do play better than this.

They win. Predictably they win, and the next frame too. We take the third because Hazel plays like a genius and I don't have the chance to drag her down. Everyone else has fun and I feel like a complete dickhead.

Good on you, Haze, Len says. *I haven't seen you play like that for a while. Eddie Bloody Charlton wouldn't have stood a chance.*

When the going gets tough … she says.

Well, I'd say honours are about even, Len goes on. *I reckon we should stop now before Haze really gets on a roll.*

It's still warm outside, warm and almost silent and lit

by a bright moon. We walk slowly. I don't want her to go, and she seems in no hurry. We stop at the roadside. She looks down and then looks up at me, into my face and I see the moon in her eyes. She says nothing.

I usually play better than that, I tell her.

I'm sure you do. She smiles.

Another long time passes with nothing said.

I might come to the markets tomorrow and see you.

That'd be good.

Maybe we could do something later.

Yeah.

Good. Any idea what?

What?

What we could do.

No. Whatever. I don't mind.

Good. Well, we will then.

Yeah.

But this is not what I want to talk about with her, this is not the conversation I want to have, this negotiating of practicalities.

So I ask her, what's going on with us?

And of course it comes out in some rude-awful way.

What do you mean?

I just wondered what you thought about what's going on with us.

She smiles again. *You're very analytical, aren't you?*

Yeah.

She gives a small laugh. *I like you. I like being with you. You're very funny, particularly when you're being very serious.*

Thanks.

No, I like that. You're very different. And you're really nice.

Nice? Nice is a death sentence. Nice people get nowhere.

Not always.

She puts her hand on my cheek, moves it behind my head, draws me towards her and kisses me on the mouth. My surprised mouth that was not quite ready for this, that was about to talk again perhaps, talk like some stupid boy. She puts her arms around me, smiles, kisses me again and her nose ring presses against my upper lip. I reach out to hold her too and I feel her body press against me as her open mouth meets mine.

A car comes over the hill and catches us in its head-lights and the moment is gone.

I'll see you tomorrow, she says, walking round to the driver's side of the car.

Yeah.

She drives away, over the low hill, and her brake lights disappear.

23

My head spins all night. All night I lie here in this totally empty house, staring up at the dark. I'm sure I don't sleep, but I must.

The doors are locked but I listen for noises. I play no music tonight and the only noise is the sea. And I think of the few seconds we had before the lights of the car came over the hill. I think this is only the start, and for me at least whatever happens from now will be new.

I walked inside and I felt different tonight, almost physically, even in these same old rooms. When she left there was just me here, me and the dark spaces of the night, the huge spaces of this small fibro house, like an empty house, with me as an intruder. Lost in this dark with my hair still messed by her hands, the taste of her still with me.

She's on her way home, along the unlit roads out to Little Mountain, to her own room. I don't know what it means to her, all of this. Can she remember my body, right up against hers?

I lie on my unmade bed. I'm used to the nights here. I've been here for hundreds of them. But none like this. None when it's just me, none so long, none with such pervasive absences of light and sound.

I try to persuade myself the night is safe, that I am safe here. That I can sleep now, heavily, deeply, dreamlessly, till morning.

24

The Caloundra markets are a favourite place of my mother's, mainly because they're not actually very good. They are not contaminated by any real notion of merit. They make no great concession to the tourist and they never have done. They sell a lot of crap there, and nobody minds.

It's light when I wake, so clearly I have slept after all. I lie there in the warming room on my already hot bed, the corner of a white sheet twisted round my legs and the rest of me uncovered.

I get up and I open the sliding doors to let some air into the house, and I make breakfast.

G'day young Alex, I hear Len's voice saying as I'm eating my toast.

I go over to the door.

Hi.

Haze and I thought we'd have a look at the markets. We wondered if you'd be interested in heading down there with us.

I finish eating and I don't tidy up. I go next door. In the car Len says, *I think I might pick myself up one of those Merv heads. What do you reckon?*

Would that be with or without the one day cricket

painted base?

I'd imagine if you were serious you'd take the base. Do you think?

As we turn into the old drive-in I see a sign that says that the markets will move at the end of the month to Corbould Park, the race track back along the road to the highway. I wonder if things will be different then, stalls in rows, people with broad hats selling goods of quality. And I think I might prefer it now, no real sense of order and a broad and comfortable range of crap.

We park among the disorder of cars and gum trees and I notice that Len, keen to do his bit for the Merv head industry, is looking out for Fortuna almost as much as I am. We see their stall and she sees us and waves.

This is Alex, Skye tells Storm. *The boy*. Storm laughs.

Alex, mate, Cliff says, offering a limp wave and not moving from his deck chair, back in the shade next to a tree. He is wearing sunglasses and gently applying aloe vera to a lump on his forehead.

Dad got stung by a bee, Fortuna says. *And he's not good with bees, so he's taking it easy today.*

He's completely unable to lift anything if he gets stung by a bee, Skye adds, in case there's any doubt. Not that Cliff is presenting himself in a way that suggests any doubt.

I introduce Hazel and Len, and Cliff does the embarrassing *Any friend of Alex's is a friend of mine* remark. Fortuna gives him a look.

I hear there are some Merv heads to be had around these parts, Len says. He makes his selection, choosing a medium size head with green zinc on the face and mad eyes and a base that will complement it appropriately. *You know,* he says, *you should think about doing a few of these with famous historical people with hair that stood up. Einstein, you know, people like that.*

Or Don King, the boxing promoter, I suggest.

Or Kramer from Seinfeld, Fortuna says slowly.

Yeah! Yeah! Cliff shouts, as though he has just been struck by a vision of religious magnitude. *Yeah, and you could put them all together in a set. Yeah, people would go for that. What do you reckon, Big?*

Yeah. Great idea, Dad.

Said with a particular lack of enthusiasm and a resigned shake of the head, but Cliff isn't noticing anything like that. He's on a roll, already talking on and gesticulating imaginatively with the hand that isn't rubbing aloe vera on his lump.

Or how about this? he says. *How about a series of famous bald people, and you grow the hair on them? How about that? Kojak, Yul Brynner, Telly Savalas.*

And a dribble of aloe vera slides down into his left eye.

Go easy on him, Fortuna says. *He's just been stung by a bee and he's not well.*

Some people stop to buy candles and honey and she tells me she'll be taking a break in twenty minutes and I should come back then.

I walk around slowly, as though I'm looking at the stalls intently, but most of the time I'm not. Past leather stubbie holders, religious icons, cacti, second-hand anything, food smells, fragrance smells. I find the stall that must be the place my mother buys chutney, and I realise I have made no plans for dinner.

I look at the satay sauce, which I think my mother has used before, but I can't think what I'd do with it.

106

The woman behind the trestle table tells me I could use it like any satay sauce. She clearly has no understanding of my needs. I decide I will go down the road and buy a burger tonight, and I thank her and move on.

Twenty minutes is starting to look like a long time when Fortuna appears beside me, takes my hand almost before I know she's there, and twists her fingers around mine.

My mother came back sooner than I expected, she says.

We buy crepes and cover them with syrup and icing sugar and sit on a log just away from the crowd.

I ask her about the markets moving and she says, *We'll be fine. We'll move and we'll see how it goes.* She shrugs her shoulders. *Anyway, it's not all we do.*

I look at her eating, talking, licking the syrup from her fingers. All the colours of her face, the icing sugar powdering around her lips. I imagine her face very close to mine. And she's looking at me, looking all over my face with those green eyes.

I want to see you later, she says. *I want to come down and see you later, okay?*

25

In the afternoon the storm clouds come in. In from the west like a dark hand, a bunched fist of lightning and rain pushing in front of the sun, making no noise at all, growing larger. The cicadas sing as though it's evening and the birds cry and go home.

Fortuna arrives as the first warm globs of water smack down onto the roof, and she runs in with one arm over her head, the rain bursting from her skin.

Made it, she says.

I turn off the cricket and I make tea. The rain intensifies in an instant, crashes over the roof, covers the veranda with wet black circles that quickly coalesce and a cold wind tears out from under the cloud, cleaning the dead leaves from the trees and the grass and spinning them away. The first thunder pounds like a distant gun and lightning cuts the inland sky.

This is suddenly a shelter here, this house, a place that keeps just the two of us from the storm. We sit at the pine dining table, each with our cup of tea, and we look out into the furious hypnotic rain.

I'm glad we're inside, she says. *Last summer we had storms like this just about every day. And they'd always break when I was half-way home from school on my bike.*

We talk about school and I tell her about catching the train, being the prefect on the train, and even as I'm saying it it sounds as though I am describing something that is long ago or far away for both of us, as though it's another country I've seen sometimes in vivid dreams. And this is quite unlike any previous ninth of January in my life, all the other years when the reality of school was merely suspended. This year it's over. Today it's over. It's something outside this rain and in my past. If I ever go back there it will be different, the grass will be different and the red brick buildings, and anything even slightly the same will catch me by surprise.

Fortuna has never had the same affinity with schools. She tells me about school in various parts of the north and then down here.

I never fitted in down here, she says. *It never really worked out that way. I don't think they thought I thought the same things were important. If you know what I mean. There was a big surf thing happening, and I like catching waves, but I was never into it the way the others were. I was never part of it. I could have been, maybe, but I don't know that I ever really wanted to be. I couldn't see the point. And I had Gail and Cliffie and the twins of course, so I thought I was okay. I always had them, wherever we moved, so that was good. It meant there was always somewhere I fitted in, without having to change a thing. I couldn't see why I'd have to change into something stupid only to impress people who were stupid, so they'd like me. That's all pretty dumb I suppose, really.*

No. No it's good you didn't let it get to you. And it's good you didn't change just because of other people. A lot of people would. I might. I don't know, but I might.

I might change to make people like me. I think I'd have found it hard at school if people hadn't liked me.

Did you change to make me like you?

Change into someone who could fix a car for example? I would have had no idea what to change into. I just saw you, you and your board and your car. And I just told myself I had nothing to lose.

She laughs, just a small laugh. She likes this, and she knows I didn't go into it thinking I had nothing to lose.

She wants me to play the Frente EP, and we turn it up, above the rain. We lie on a bean bag near the portable CD player and she listens intently. She closes her eyes.

Play the last two songs again, she says when it finishes.

So I do, and I lie beside her, on my side quite close beside her, watching her, watching her delicate closed eyes, her breasts lifting just a little with each slow breath, her long bare legs crossed at the ankles.

She looks incredibly peaceful, here with me, under the thrashing rain.

I play the songs again, and again, and I don't know how many times before she opens her eyes.

She looks me over, as though I've just arrived. She rolls to face me, puts her left arm over me, closes her eyes again and we kiss, one long slow kiss until a while after the end of the CD.

Outside, the rain is fading now and there is a cool silver light slipping through the clouds.

I'd better go, she says. *While the weather's like this. It could get worse again and I might not be able to get home.*

She looks at me, close up and carefully, as though

110

she is saying much more than observations about weather. As though *worse again* mightn't be such a bad thing.

I walk with her to the door and I watch her run across the drenched grass, kicking water from the wide puddles, her left arm over her head again to keep back the rain.

Some time later my mother calls, to see how I'm going, to see how the storm was up here.

I tell her fine, I'm fine, the storm was fine. There are no problems.

I go to sleep to the sound of rain, the tired storm doing another sweep overhead, blowing itself out in the dark, throwing the last of its rain across our roof, like an old hand now, and able to do no harm.

STORM POEM

Just us
Here
Behind the storm wall

This keeps us in
Keeps them out
Keeps them a perfect invisible distance away
Behind the bars
Of the rain

26

Big reckons you're going to be a lawyer, Cliff says, as he looks critically over some plates he has just fired, dinner-sized with tropical coastscapes, vivid blues and greens for the sea and sky and rainforested hills, tiny white houses with red roofs.

Well, not necessarily. I might not get in.

I'm back sitting on the box, the visitor's box-seat in Cliff's workshop. My hair is still a little damp from swimming and Fortuna is elsewhere, stuffing stockings to make Merv heads. Cliff is wearing his working vest again, and again nothing else, and he shuffles around the workshop with clay dried to powder over his thighs and his arms, leaning over things and looking at them.

When will you know?

It's the twentieth it's in the paper, so that's, what, ten days? Late next week.

Yeah. I went to Queensland Uni you know. Did Big tell you that? Bachelor of Arts. First six months of 1971. Great place.

You didn't stay though.

No. Brisbane in 1971 wasn't the place for me, so I travelled and I never quite got round to going back. I'm sure it's a different place now though, Brisbane and the

112

Uni. I'm sure they're both different. Some of the people I travelled with went back. One of them even did Law.

Really?

Yeah. He did something else first, and then he did Law. He came to tell me he was going to. I don't know if he was looking for me to approve, or what. As if it'd bother me if someone did Law, or didn't. We were living in northern New South Wales then and he drove down for a week or two and helped us pick avocados, I think. Something like that. It was a while ago. Anyway, the last time I saw him he was wearing sandals and shorts and no shirt and driving an old Jeep and telling me the important things you can do with a law degree. That was ten or fifteen years ago. I wondered how he was going with the important things, and then I saw him on TV a couple of years ago in a pin-stripe suit, defending some white-collar criminal. I think the agenda had changed a bit, and I guess that's fine, if it's making him happy, but you've got to wonder where he really stood, years ago.

He stops and looks at me and gives me a half-smile.

And that seems to be that.

I help him put the plates into wooden boxes, resting each one on a bed of dried grass.

Alex, Fortuna says from the doorway when we've almost finished, *do you want to help me get lunch?*

I go with her to the kitchen and we wash fruit and put it on the table with honey and bread.

I think your father thinks I shouldn't be doing Law, I tell her.

Really? Why?

He told me a story about someone. Someone who did a law degree and seemed to change a lot. Into something your father didn't like.

113

Really. I don't think that means you shouldn't. I don't think that's necessarily him telling you you shouldn't.

Do you think I shouldn't? Do you think it's a problem, me planning to do Law?

No, no. Why would it be? Why did you say that? Why would I have a problem with you doing Law? Do you have a problem with me not doing Law?

No. No not at all.

Good. Good. Then she looks less serious. *Then no one has any problems. And I'm sure that's not what my father was saying. Did you get those plates boxed?*

Yeah.

Good. We've got an order through for some more. Mum said someone in Noosa just faxed us.

You have a fax?

Yeah.

Your father has a go at people who own pin-stripe suits and he owns a fax?

Cliffie will never admit to owning a fax, so that's the important difference. He will never, ever, feel good about owning a fax. So he pretends it doesn't exist, that it's my mother's business. He hates it. He hates the idea that the easiest thing for him to do is to sell to Noosa, to fuddle around here working without any hurry, while my mother receives the faxes that tell him what to make. In his perfect world if someone liked his plate, they would give him a bag of potatoes and two chickens. Here he has to make do with money, and he finds that very uncomfortable.

This is not easy to work out.

I never told you it would be easy to work out. Dad likes you. I have no idea what he thinks of your course preferences, but he likes you. Okay?

114

The rest of the family turns up for lunch and I meet Fortuna's mother, Gail, for the first time. She looks older than Cliff, and perhaps she is, and she has hair like all her daughters.

Finally, she says. *The young man I've heard so much about.*

Skye laughs.

There is something about Gail that means lunch seems to happen around her. She takes the first plate and Cliff cuts her two thick slices of bread without saying a thing. He then cuts two for himself and puts the knife down.

You'll be working hard, Cliffie, she's saying, and she uncrumples a sheet of fax paper from her pocket. *Lovely Lionel's after you again.*

Cliff almost groans there and then under the weight of the impending work.

She turns to me, looks up from the honey she's spreading across her bread and says, *So Alex, tell me about yourself. Tell me the things I don't know.*

As though I am to present my credentials.

Right at this moment I feel I don't have any, and I feel as though I don't fit in, as though I don't understand this lunch so I can't fit in. I feel welcome and strange at the same time.

After lunch, the others start to clear the table and Gail stops me when I stand up to help.

There's really not much to do, she says. *Come and have a cup of tea.*

We go outside and sit on the veranda. She holds her tea in both hands and I notice signs of surgery on one arm, a big blood vessel pounding near a long scar. I try hard to look somewhere else.

115

Big says it's just you and your mother.

Yeah.

You must be very important to her then.

Well, I've never really thought about it. I suppose we're important to each other.

Yeah, I'm sure you are. She stops and laughs. *We should make light conversation, shouldn't we? It's just that my daughter is very important to me and I think I'm trying to convince myself that you're a fit and proper person for her to spend time with. And I realise that's completely unfair. I can't believe I could even think of becoming that kind of parent. So just reassure me. Tell me that you don't deal in or take dangerous drugs, that you don't molest animals and that you won't knowingly or wilfully do my daughter harm.*

All of the above.

Well I'm glad that's out of the way.

If you want I can provide references from teachers and lifelong family friends.

Good idea. Get them to fax me. She laughs again. *Sorry Alex. I'm such a bloody parent, aren't I?*

Yeah. So's my mother. I know the score. Like she says, *It's a dangerous world out there, and you can never be too careful.*

You can never be too careful. It's crazy isn't it?

Sometimes.

Cliff appears at the door and says, *Alex, have you got any plans this afternoon? You're not doing anything, are you?* And he's saying this quietly, and I can't imagine why. All I can do is go along with it.

No. I don't think so.

Do you like music?

Yes.

116

Good. Come with me. He turns to Fortuna who is still behind him in the kitchen. *Big, mind if I borrow Alex for a bit?*

What do you mean?

I just thought I'd take him down the back, you know.

Dad ... Said in a way that makes it sound like a caution to a pet about to misbehave.

He said he liked music.

Has he explained this to you, Alex?

Not yet.

We've got a bit of a studio down there. I just thought you might like to see it, that's all.

You don't have to go, Alex, Fortuna says.

No, no. I'd like to.

Dad, he's just being polite.

No, I'd like to go.

Dad, if you make him go, you have to promise not to tell him any boring stories, okay?

Cliff's mind is already down at the studio, so he just says, *Yeah yeah*, and leads me across a cleared area of bush to a separate building. Inside, the walls are covered with egg cartons and there's a drum kit already set up, a few guitars, a sax, keyboards. He takes me to an old machine with several knobs and dials.

Four-track, he says, twiddling a few of the knobs affectionately. *Still as honest as the day it was made.*

He picks up an acoustic guitar and records several different versions of 'Norwegian Wood', all the time fixing me with a quite fiendish glare while singing lines about once having a girl, or her once having him.

And then there's backing vocals of course, he says enthusiastically. *Just hang on a tick.*

He comes back with Fortuna, who looks less enthusiastic and says, *He's not doing 'Norwegian Wood', is he?* Shaking her head and rolling her eyes.

Yeah.

It's the song of the moment. He goes through phases. Sometimes it's Dylan, sometimes ...

Okay Big, Cliff says, ignoring all this, *from the usual bit. From 'She asked me to stay'.*

Yeah. Sorry Alex. I'll take you home after this, if you want. She puts on the headphones and says, *Let me hear it.* Cliff asks if the key is okay and she thinks her way through the lines and says, *Yeah, yeah. I think I can get there.*

So she sings, she nods in time with the first few lines and she puts one hand on the headphones and the other on her thigh and she takes a breath and sings. And Cliff switches the sound so Fortuna hears the parts already recorded and we hear only her, her voice filling the room all by itself as it makes some strangely absent harmony.

Cliff grins at me and says, *She's good, isn't she?*

I don't need to answer. For me, this is the sort of thing I would like to dream at night, but never seem to.

By now Cliff will not be stopped. He opens the door and shouts for Gail and the twins.

Are we going to do a few numbers, Dad? Skye says, grinning at me as she walks in.

She slings the bass over her shoulder and plugs it in, and Storm blows a few notes on the sax.

The upright or the Roland? Gail says. *What are we starting with?*

'Spicks and Specks', Skye says quickly.

Cliff agrees. *Good choice. You know this one, Alex?*

I don't think so.

It's early Bee Gees, but don't let that put you off. It's got a great feel.

Gail sits down at the upright piano, and Fortuna moves behind the drums, smiles unconvincingly, says, *Am I on?* to her mike. She beats maybe eight times on the same drum, then Skye joins in on bass, then Gail, thumping one chord repeatedly before breaking into the melody, and the song sounds vaguely familiar after all.

Next, Gail moves to the electronic keyboard and they do 'Echo Beach', with Fortuna singing lead while still playing drums. And all this time I sit on a stool, wondering what my life is becoming, wondering how I came to be chosen to be this audience of one. This is just another item on the growing list of things I am unlikely to tell the people I went to school with when I see them next. *So what did you do at the coast?* Well, one day I sat on a stool in the hinterland and a hippy family played pop songs for me.

The pop songs aren't over. Cliff starts doing something quite country on guitar, and it becomes Vika and Linda Bull's 'When Will You Fall for Me?'. Fortuna sings lead again and Storm and Skye do backing vocals, and when they reach the end they keep singing, chorus after chorus just with their three voices, trying different harmonies, different tempos, like clever old soul singers, finding unexpected resonances. They finally stop, and laugh.

That was great, Cliff says. *What did you think, Alex?*

Yeah. Great, really good.

So, do you sing?

Me? No.

I think you might, Fortuna says. *I think you might be about to.*

119

No, I don't think so.

Come over here, Cliff says.

He walks to the piano, and the others move in a way that seems to herd me over there too.

Just a few notes, he says. *A few notes after I play them. Just lah.*

You want me to go lah after you play a note?

Yeah.

I don't know if I can do that.

Sure you can.

He plays the first note. I lah. *Good.* He plays another. I lah again. If I felt silly sitting on the stool I feel much worse now.

Alex, you're fine, Fortuna says. *You're in tune.*

Really?

Keep going.

So Cliff plays more notes and I keep lahing.

Good, he says, and he turns to the others with a knowing smile. *This is it. This is our boy.*

And he looks at me and nods, as though I know too. But I don't. I say nothing, and I think I give him the smile of fear, or at least uncertainty.

Undeterred, he rummages around in an old cardboard box until he finds a cassette, which he holds up to me like a lost treasure.

Here it is, he says, and he loads it into a player. *This is the Housemartins, doing an* a capella *version of the song 'Caravan of Love'. You only got this if you bought the album early and got the bonus EP. We've been waiting for the right voice to come along to sing lead. We all know our parts.*

I don't know if I'm up to these responsibilities, but he's saying this in a very earnest way, and he plays it, rewinds it and plays it again. And the others do know their parts, and they sing along. Then they start without the tape, all looking at me, ready for me, Fortuna, I think, only just managing not to laugh at my visible struggle with probably the most acutely embarrassing moment of my life.

Just when I wonder what I'm going to do, how I'm going to handle this, I start to sing, line after line about someone being ready, ready for the time of their life.

And Cliff tells me, *Let it swing, just a bit, let it go*, and for the next hour or two we do 'Caravan of Love' until we all know it's absolutely perfect. We record and Cliff plays it back and says, *That is just magic. Bloody beautiful.* And he grins and slaps me on the shoulder. *Let's go and make some dinner.*

And I haven't noticed the afternoon go, but outside it's cooling down and the sun is settling into the trees. We make lentil soup, and I've only heard of lentil soup before. We eat it with some of Cliff's bread, which he offers to teach me to make, and he gives me a glass of his lychee wine.

It's very cold, he says, *because it's best if it's very cold.*

Don't do it, Alex, Fortuna says. *Better people than you have tried the lychee wine and died an awful death.*

I sip it. It's sweet and strange and certainly not good.

Unfortunately it's the '93, Cliff says, *So you're not seeing it at its best. Not the best year, '93.*

After dinner Fortuna drives me home. We sit in the car outside my house.

It's dark in there, she says.

Yeah.

121

She is humming, and tapping the steering wheel slowly. She sings quietly, the line from 'Caravan of Love' about being ready.

She leans over and we kiss and we know she should go. We know I should go inside and she should go.

Can't have Cliffe thinking I'm killing myself on Sugarbag Road, she says, still close and quiet.

So I get out and stand by the kerb and I watch her drive away, listen to her drive to the end of the street and turn and then keep driving, off into the night.

I stumble through the dark rooms of the house, the lychee wine still kicking away in my head, along with the songs. And I'm ready, I'm ready, maybe.

27

It's not until the morning that I notice the toilet is filling strangely. I notice in the morning because that's when it overflows. Only a little, certainly, but I suspect in my mother's mind there would be no such thing as an insignificant toilet overflow.

I'm not sure what I should do. I stare at it for a while, but the puddle grows neither smaller nor larger. The level in the bowl lowers slowly. I clean the floor and the situation seems at least stable.

So I go for a swim.

I catch a few waves, but my mind is on the plumbing the whole time. I walk up the beach to the house wondering if I will be met by a tide of effluent running through our garden and down to the sea. The last several days of flushings swirling around me as people walk past, getting to know a side of me I'd rather keep to myself.

This doesn't happen. The toilet looks fine. I flush again in case it is fine and the water surges up and spills over onto the floor. The new puddle is quite large. It's clear I have a problem. I can imagine water creeping between lino floor tiles and rotting weight-bearing beams, rotting away important parts of the house while my mother isn't here. While it's entrusted to me. I find a couple of old towels and do my best to mop up.

I go next door and explain it to Len who comes to have a look. He is smart enough not to flush and tells me we'll call Fred Brahms and he'll sort it out. *Better off leaving this sort of thing to the experts. He fixed up our en suite and that was no picnic. He was in the services you know, navy. Fiery I think they called him. Interesting bloke. Bloody good plumber though.*

Fred Brahms is out on a job, but as a favour to Len his wife says she'll send him over straight after lunch.

I call my mother, knowing she will be out at work, and I leave a message on our answering machine telling her about the problem, and that Len is now involved and it'll be sorted out today.

S'pose we might as well play some pool, Len says.

The standard of my play is sufficiently different from a few nights ago that he comments. We play two close frames, and I take the second when Len fouls at a critical moment.

I go home to check that the crisis hasn't worsened. The toilet looks deceptively fine. I call Fortuna.

Where have you been? she says.

Over next door.

She's been calling while I've been playing pool with Len. I tell her about the toilet and she says she'll come down and wait with me after lunch.

The phone rings when I put it down. *Where have you been?* my mother begins, as though she has been listening. *Where were you last night?*

At Fortuna's. I had dinner there. She dropped me home after. Did you get the message on the machine?

No. I haven't been home.

There's a bit of a problem with the toilet. A minor sort of overflow. Len had a look at it and he's got a plumber coming round this afternoon.

There is a pause, the kind of pause offered to a liar before the accusation is made.

You're out all night and now you're breaking the toilet? What are you trying to flush down there?

Just the usual. And I wasn't out all night. Look, everything's fine. I'm having a good time. Everything's fine except the toilet, which would have happened anyway. I've been swimming, playing pool, all the usual things. I'm learning to make bread.

Why I said that I don't know. I think it was all I could salvage from the day before that wouldn't seem crazy. I thought it would make me sound really normal, stable, safe. I thought she would like it.

That's really nice. You'll have to make me some sometime.

I think I'll need some more practice first.

So now I am actually lying she's believing every word of it. I think I'm going to have to learn to make the bread.

What's it like? What sort of bread is it?

It's like restaurant bread, you know, bread in a flower pot for $4.50. That sort of thing. Very cool bread, but I'm still only learning, from Fortuna's father.

The lie gets bigger, my nose gets longer. Still only learning I said though. I emphasised that. I think I'm covered.

Let me know what happens with the plumber, she says. *And you'll have to make me some of your bread soon.*

Yeah. Sure.

She lets me go, happier with me now, the bread somehow a symbol that I'm not being too corrupted when I'm beyond her reach. The bread also another expectation that I'll have to live up to. Why does she make me say these things?

Fred Brahms wears overalls and an old white T-shirt and calls me Mr Delaney. Whatever I say, he doesn't stop calling me Mr Delaney, so I call him Mr Brahms. He stands staring at the apparently normal toilet asking probing questions about its malfunction.

Roots it'll be, tree roots, he says. *Where are your pipes?*

Out the back maybe, I tell him, and it's clear to both of us I have no idea.

But they'd run off straight to the sea that way, Mr Delaney. My guess is they're heading in the opposite direction.

So we proceed to the side of the house where the pipe from the toilet drops to the ground. We are inspecting the site when Fortuna arrives.

Hi, she says, looking at the two of us watching the grass intently.

Afternoon, Mrs Delaney. Fred Brahms is the name. He shakes her hand.

Hi, she says again, trying to conceal a smirk. *I'm not actually Mrs Delaney. I'm just a friend. Of Mr Delaney's.*

Ah, just friends. He glares at us as though we are the

devil's henchpeople. *I reckon it'll be just here, Mr Delaney. I'll just get some gear from the truck.*

So when did we get married? Fortuna says when he's gone.

It must have been last night, the lychee wine. There are several hours that are just a blur. I can remember singing, and food. Could have been a wedding.

Who is this guy?

Look, I know he's bizarre, but he's going to allow me to flush the toilet again.

He comes back down the driveway carrying a spade and several pieces of equipment I can't identify. He drops them to the ground and stops to wipe sweat from his forehead with his beefy left forearm.

Can I get you a drink, Mr Brahms? I suggest.

That'd be great. Just water, mind. You can never have too much water on a day like today.

I go upstairs with Fortuna and she says she'll have to stay up here or she'll laugh. I take Mr Brahms his drink. He is already at work.

Ta. Much appreciated. He drinks half the glass at a gulp. *So what do you do for a crust, Mr Delaney? Work in Caloundra do you?*

No, I'm a student still.

At the university eh? That's a good start that is. It's a good idea these days. Get yourself a ticket. Mind you, a lot of these youngsters aren't really up to it today, are they? You hear about 'em all the time. Drugs and violence and fornication. You wouldn't hear of it in my day, not with decent people. Sex is for procreation, not for entertainment, that's what I say. And if we could all just live by that the world'd be a far far better place.

And he fixes me with a stare, drives a stare right

128

through me and almost pins me to the wall with it.

There certainly are a lot of problems, I manage to say eventually.

And fornication's at the root of most of 'em, you mark my words.

And still the reinforced steel stare as though I'm fornicating now, right in front of him, putting one away with this girl who isn't Mrs Delaney

I'll bear that in mind, I tell him, and start retreating for the stairs.

You do that.

When I'm upstairs again I feel like I'm hiding for the rest of the time he's there, hiding in my own house, hoping the floors don't creak under my feet and remind him of fornication.

I tell Fortuna everything he's said and she says, *But what if I can't hold myself back*, and she pulls me over onto a bean bag and starts an orgasm performance like Meg Ryan in *When Harry Met Sally*. Squirming and moaning with Fred Brahms just metres away and probably listening to every unholy panting syllable.

Please, please, I say in a way that comes out in an awful puritanical hiss, not now. And I clamp my hand over her mouth. I can feel her smiling, hear her laughing through her nose. She prises my fingers away.

Funny boy, she says, still laughing at me.

At ground level, Fred Brahms whistles on tunelessly. I hear him flush the downstairs toilet and he comes up to tell me, *It's all fine now, Mr Delaney*. And he hands me an account, which includes a deduction of ten percent as a student discount.

You might like to read this, he says, giving me a photocopied pamphlet. *It's from the scriptures.*

I thank him and he goes. Fortuna takes it from me.

It's all about sin, she says. *I wonder why he gave it to you. You don't sin, do you Alex?*

Hardly at all. I think I don't sin enough.

She says, *Let's go for a walk*, and we go down to the beach and she takes my hand.

I'll be away most of tomorrow.

What are you doing?

Taking my mother to Brisbane. She's got to see a doctor. I don't think I've told you about this yet. She's had a kidney transplant, that's why we came down here, when she got sick. She's fine now, but she just needs to go for follow up. She had her blood tests last week, so tomorrow she has to go to the clinic at the hospital. I think it'll be fine. She feels fine.

Are you fine?

Yeah. I'll be better when it's over tomorrow.

It's good that you take her to Brisbane. She must appreciate not just going by herself.

Yeah, she does. But she couldn't go by herself anyway. She doesn't drive.

Really?

Yeah. She says she's philosophically opposed to the idea of licencing. She's always said that. She made me get one of course, and Dad's got one. I think she's just a very, very bad driver. Anyway, Dad's not good at dealing with these things, so it's better if I take her. And that's where you come in, if that's okay.

Sure. What do I do?

You just have to be with him. Storm and Skye won't hang around, 'cause it just makes them more worried. They'll probably come to the beach, so it'd be good if you could stay with him, keep him

130

occupied. Could you do that?

Sure. I hope it all goes okay.

Yeah.

And the concern shows in her face all of a sudden and she stops walking, looks at the sand and then back at me, and moves in against my arm, presses her face into my chest and holds me.

You're very important to them, I say.

And maybe there are lots of things I could have said, but that's the one that came out. Straight out of the conversation with her mother yesterday. *My daughter is very important to me.* That line. And my version sounds stupid to me even as I say it, but she's not really listening anyway. She's just holding on.

She wipes her eyes on my sleeve and smiles and says, *Let's go for a swim.*

29

G'day mate, Cliff says when he comes to the door, his face a mixture of concern and disguise.

We will pretend this is normal, fine, that it's Cliff who drops over just about every day and not his daughter. He's fiddling with the car keys, not quite certain what happens next. He's waiting for my lead. I don't have a lead.

It's a good looking day, I say.

Yeah.

How are you going with those plates?

Got a few more to do.

Do you want a hand?

Yeah. Good.

Now we have a purpose. We can work and pretend that's what we're doing together. We get into the car like workers, talking plates and boxes and things.

This is the first time I've driven with Cliff, and he handles a car the way he handles a conversation, like a man who has little respect for the enforced discipline of roads. And he chats as he goes, his arms doing more talking than driving, pointing out the features of what he sees as a blighted landscape.

Look at it, mate, it's beautiful, and look what they're

132

doing to it. Beau Vista, Heritage bloody Chase, Street of bloody Dreams. Sounds like a bloody theme park, not a place where you'd live. Bloody brick houses all crammed in with a few bits of painted wood arranged on them in some pathetic attempt at a federation metaphor. Heritage, federation, colonial, what a bunch of crap, he says, punching the wheel. *Do you see Henry Parkes lining up to buy one of those brick boxes? Urban sprawl is what it is, mate.*

We turn down Sunset Drive and the road becomes graded dirt with bush on either side.

And this'll go too, all this. Future Urban we're zoned along here. Don't know where we'll go then. We'll sell to some bastard for some incredible amount of money and he'll put in two hundred town houses with synthetic grass tennis courts and a pool with a dolphin motif in dark tiles on the bottom and a gazebo and a sauna. And there'll be working bees and rules about how long you can hang your laundry out for and monthly get-togethers poolside where they'll all settle down for a few beers and a sausage sizzle and talk about computer software. It's bloody offensive, the lot of it.

He takes out a small tree with the bullbar as we career along the track to the house and he doesn't even seem to notice, even though his head snaps back with the impact. At least it doesn't stop him talking. He slams the car door as though it has a developer's head in it, and I follow him into the house.

Beer? he says, drawing two unlabelled bottles from the fridge by their necks. *Home brew.* And he flicks the tops off with a bottle opener and gives me one. *It's different, more like Guinness really. I don't know why though; it just worked out that way. Hope you like it.*

133

It's not even nine in the morning and of course the beer has a kick like a soccer hooligan. Soon even the spill-over effect of Cliff's tension means nothing to me. He's still tense, but I'm quite calm and warm in the patchy sun under the trees, sitting on a log and trying to drink slowly. He's talking on, talking out to the clearing about the land and what it means to him.

He stops and turns to me, a serious, worried look all across his face.

Sometimes I get scared I'll lose her, mate, he says. *And then what would I do? What would I do?* I can't say anything to this. I feel completely powerless. *This is my life, Gail, the kids. That's it. Most of the time people don't know how lucky they are, mate. But I do. I couldn't be luckier. I went off all those years ago on that ridiculous journey to find myself and I found her. You couldn't get luckier than that. Gail and three glorious daughters. What a bloody life. What did I ever do to deserve it? There's no one in the world luckier than me, mate. That's why I get scared.*

She'll be all right though, won't she? Things are going fine, aren't they? It's amazing what they can do now.

Good on you, mate. I just love her so much. And he takes another large mouthful of beer and looks into the distance. *Mate, when we met there was all that free love thing going on, and I reckon we both had lots of very free love, you know. But when I saw her I thought, that's all I want. I just looked at her and I thought I've got to talk to that girl. And I just said the stupidest things. I got myself so tense I could hardly breathe when I went up to talk to her, and I think I said something like, Hey, want some bananas? Like I was just about to die of asthma, and she laughed. It's a hell of a laugh mate, it only made things much worse.*

Yeah. I know the feeling.

Yeah. Another beer? I show him my bottle and he seems surprised that there could still be nearly half of it left. *It's not in limited supply you know.*

I'm just not used to it.

Sure. I am, so I might have another. Then we might get to work and make some yuppie bait. A few more of those elegant tropical plates. He burps and laughs and slaps me on the shoulder when I stand.

We go inside and he transfers a few beers to the fridge in the workshop, in case I change my mind. With the beer and his other preoccupations he forgets to drop his pants and change into his work vest. This is a bit of a relief, for while I am now okay with the idea of him working as he does, I would be a little less comfortable actually being there for the process of changing, just me and a middle-aged man in a room in the bush, while he takes his clothes off. Sometimes I feel very hung-up and middle class.

He drops the clay on the wheel and works.

So, you like Big, he says.

Yeah.

Good. She likes you too.

Good.

We all do. I like you. He glances up at me and throws another lump of clay onto the wheel. I'm not sure if I'm supposed to say something. I'm not sure what he means. He works the clay, squeezes it and twists it and shapes it. *I don't think she's ever liked anyone like this before.*

Never anyone like me?

No, at all. Like this. She's never been in this position.

Oh.

And you know I like you. And this is beginning to sound like a mafia conversation before someone gets killed. *But I'm her father you know.*

Yeah.

And she's my daughter.

Yeah.

And I want to say to him Cliff, it's okay, I've done this already. Gail cleared me yesterday. But I think he has his own struggle to get through.

And I'm not used to this, this stuff, okay? And he's pounding the clay with a closed fist and then stroking it firmly upwards, pounding and stroking. I can't see this becoming a plate. It's a very large lump of clay now, and it's tending to the vertical. *She's never had an interest like this before, and it's great it's you. I'm glad it's someone I like. That's great. You understand that, don't you? You know what I mean?*

Not completely.

Okay, okay, okay. He's very tense about having to spell it out, whatever it is, and the clay is rising into a column, like a thick forearm, with a fist on the end. Not a plate, nothing like a plate. *All right, what I mean is, it's okay. Whatever, whatever.* Staring right at me saying *whatever* as though he's said it all now, clearly, emphatically. And he's caressing the fist part of the clay, caressing it and squeezing more clay up from the base, turning the fist into the head of a club, the head of a snake. *What I mean is, it's between the two of you, okay? It's up to you. I've been through all this, I've been young, I know, okay?* Stopping, looking at me, working the clay. *And I like you, I want you to know that I like you. And that whatever happens it's got to be your*

136

choice, and I'm cool, okay? Whatever the two of you decide to do, whatever you want, it's fine by me. And I think it's great. And the column of clay is a towering penis, fifty, sixty centimetres tall and perilously unstable, coiling and flexing in his fingers, flailing around like some dangerous weapon of love. *Whatever,* he says one more time, and he takes his hands from the clay and offers them to me palms up to give me *whatever* and the frightening phallus collapses, buckles mid-shaft and tumbles into his lap, striking his shorts with enough impact to make him wince.

Thanks, I say, because I gather gratitude is in order. He seems to have endured some painful dilemma on my behalf, and not just in his shorts.

But I can't sit here, I can't sit here on this box with this frantic clay-trousered man who seems to be talking about me, his daughter and sex. This is all too big, this whole issue, bigger almost than when he makes it in clay, all too much just now. It's not as though it hasn't crossed my mind, but I think it's very different, the way we look at this, Cliff and Fred Brahms and me. And I can't say to him, every time your daughter touches me I feel incredible, because I don't think he'd understand. I think he'd make assumptions. I can't explain it to him, any of it. I can't explain it to myself.

Could you show me how to make bread now? I ask him instead.

Sure, sure. Just be careful, okay. You know? With the other thing? You'll be careful?

Yeah.

His second beer seems to have vanished into him at some point during the discussion, though at the time neither of us noticed, so he takes a third from the fridge when we're back in the kitchen. He places his hands on the bench, some distance apart, takes a few deep breaths, and thinks about bread.

The phone rings. He looks at me, fearfully.

Could you get it, mate?

I pick it up and it's Fortuna.

Everything's fine, she says. *Totally fine. They were really pleased with Mum's results. It couldn't have been better.*

Great.

I turn and grin and nod to Cliff and give him a thumbs up. Fortuna's still talking.

How's Dad?

Fine. Really good. We're about to make bread.

He's pissed, isn't he?

Well, yeah, but he's fine.

He hasn't done anything embarrassing, has he? He's got an embarrassing mouth when he's pissed.

No, no, everything's fine. He's just had a couple of beers and we're making bread.

Just make sure he doesn't hurt himself.

And I'm watching him lean heavily on the bench, his mad grin sliding all over his face. Fortuna says they've got a couple of things to do in the city and they'll be back in two hours or so.

You'll still be there, won't you?

Yeah.

She goes, and I tell Cliff everything's great, couldn't be better, and he wipes his damp eyes and hugs me.

Thanks, mate. Let's make some bread. He opens a cupboard door and removes an alphabetised card file. *Thank God Gail's so organised, or I'd never find my recipes. I'd be useless without her, wouldn't I?* He flicks

138

through the B's. *Here we go. You'll like this one. It's from a magazine. I cut it out a year or so ago.*

I say nothing, but this is not how I had imagined the process.

We follow the recipe almost to the letter and he tells me, *There's an art to dough, and you have to know that from the start. The sifting, the mixing. This consistency is critical, okay?*

He flours up the board and we knead and he shows me just how the hands are supposed to be, takes my hands and shapes them properly.

This is where you need a bit of judgment, adding the last bit of flour. Again, it's about consistency. It can't be too sloppy, it can't be too dry and floury, and there shouldn't be any lumps, okay?

And very soon after we load this perfect dough into the pre-heated moderate oven, Cliff, his fourth bottle of beer only just begun, passes out.

Thirty to thirty five minutes, he says, ineffectually. *Or until browned.*

And then he's gone, slumped in a kitchen chair and snoring.

I watch the bread, and its smell permeates the room. I sit in this quiet tide of snoring with no other sound and I watch the bread brown. It takes forty-two minutes, and then I remove it from the oven to cool.

I cut the end off and eat it with some hommus from the fridge, and still he sleeps. It's great bread, and I've never eaten anything I've made before, not from a recipe. I try to stay awake, but maybe I doze too, sitting on another chair at the kitchen table with the beer dragging me down. Good beer. Strong beer.

Eventually I hear a car, coming at me from far away,

the Moke. I hear it park and Fortuna and Gail walk in. Cliff's head jerks up from his chest.

Christ, the bread! he shouts, and we tell him it's okay.

Fortuna takes my hand. We walk outside.

Thanks, she says, *for today and yesterday. It made a big difference.*

And I can't look at her right now, not easily. Not with this pain in my head and the bright light and the day's strange conversations. As though at any moment Cliff could loom up at a window and reaffirm his feelings, shout encouragement, make an awful mess of things.

BREAD

2½ cups plain flour
1½ cups rolled oats
2 cups wholemeal plain flour
1 teaspoon baking powder
1 teaspoon bicarbonate of soda
1 teaspoon salt
1 large egg
2 cups buttermilk

Sift two cups of plain flour into a mixing bowl. Add one cup of rolled oats, the wholemeal plain flour, baking powder, bicarbonate of soda and salt, and stir.

Beat the egg lightly, combine it with the buttermilk and add to the mixture in the mixing bowl. Stir until a dough is formed.

Knead the dough on a floured board until it is manageable but soft, adding the required amount of the remaining plain flour.

Divide the dough into two portions, each of which should be sufficient to make a small loaf. Roll each loaf in the the remaining rolled oats, place both loaves on a greased baking tray and bake at 180°C (moderate) in a pre-heated oven for 30 minutes or until browned.

Remove the loaves from the oven and allow them to cool on a rack.

30

I'm running low on food, and since all I can make is bread I organise to go shopping at Coles in the morning with Len.

We take separate trolleys and circulate and I load up with watermelon and soft drink and a selection of peculiar teas in case Fortuna might like any of them. I buy a range of dinners for one, but we don't have a microwave at the coast so that limits my options.

Near the top of my list is toilet paper, having lost several rolls with the flooding a couple of days ago. At the time, throwing out sodden unused toilet rolls seemed a trivial part of the events, but with the use of the last roll this morning my need is immediate.

I browse with my half-loaded trolley and my list in my hand and I push my way up the medicinal aisle and park until I find the Sorbent four-packs with the blue aquatic motif, the choice my mother will expect if she comes up for the weekend.

I am about to move on when I notice I have parked next to the condoms.

Saturn, Regular with nonoxynol-9. Saturn, Coloured Assortment (fragrant). Fragrant condoms. Fragrant condoms in Coles? This makes me tense. What's the fragrance? Is there colour–fragrance matching? Do the green ones smell like apple, the red ones like strawberry? *Oh how nice you bought strawberry, my favourite. Love the smell.* Or do they do something really perverse and make the blue ones smell of banana? Or are they all musk or alpine or Obsession or pheromones?

I notice that I'm holding them now, standing in Coles near my melon, my toilet paper, my selection of peculiar teas, not moving on. Holding the condoms, turning them over in my hands, reading the fine print and squishing them around in the packet without meaning to. Fragrant condoms. This doesn't make me feel good. I can't quite see the point.

Reaction — Ribbed. Reaction — Affinity. Ribbed condoms in Coles? Right near vitamin B and Bandaids. I'm not convinced you can feel the ribs through the packet.

Two years or so ago, at school, we were visited by some family planning people, doctor friends of my mother's, fearless middle-aged women. They brought all the gear with them. Pill packets set in plastic for use as paper weights, spermicides, IUDs, but mainly condoms. And they passed them out among the class in the dimly lit audiovisual room and said, *We'd like to be sure we get the IUDs back. There's not much you can do with them anyway unless you've been trained to use them. And if you could also return the pill packets and the gels and foams and creams, that'd be good too.* They knew the condoms wouldn't be coming back. They stressed lubrication and early application. They said condoms now came in infinite varieties, to suit everyone's tastes, and putting a condom on didn't have to kill the mood. It could be part of the fun. Whatever that meant. And whenever they asked questions they asked me, because mine was the only name they knew. *So, Alex, can you think of any added advantages the condom might have over other forms of contraception? So, Alex, could you tell us all why you don't put the condom on until the penis is fully erect?* Looking straight at me. Making cold merciless eye contact and making me talk about this as though I practised it at home.

Mate, I hear Len saying behind me. *I'm about ready to go.*

Yeah, me too. I was just here for the toilet rolls.

Yeah, that's fine.

No really.

Yeah, fine. You've got to have toilet paper. I think you should buy anything you might need. It makes sense. You don't want to take any chances, do you?

I'll be fine.

I flick the Reaction — Ribbed packet back onto the shelf as though it was never in my hand, I straighten the Sorbent four-pack, and I move decisively to the check-out.

On the way home we talk about the weather.

31

We walk on the beach.

Fortuna comes over and we walk slowly in the late afternoon when the air is cooler and the breeze is beginning and the light is coming in lower from the west, over the land.

We go through the shin-deep water where Tooway Creek crosses the sand and runs into the sea and we walk on the rocks of the headland.

Far out to sea two ships turn away from straight lines, head away from each other, for different parts of the horizon.

She takes my hand and leads me carefully over the wet mossy contours of the stone as though she is my eyes.

I am just behind her and watching her fingers around mine, her splashed calves, her bare arms.

I can see your house, she says, pointing, as though she's the first person to find it.

Yeah. From here it looks really close to the beach, doesn't it? I wonder how long it'll be there, the way the erosion's going. We used to have more garden. Every cyclone we have less. They put down rocks and it doesn't stop it. It might be fine for years though. It's hard to know.

From here it's even more apparent that it's only the pandanus trees and the she-oaks gripping hard to the sand that keep us any garden at all.

But I thought it would always be there, I tell her. I've moved in Brisbane, but I thought this house would always be there. Even in years when summer holidays bored me it seemed one of the few inevitable things. This house and Christmas were the only things that meant my mother and my father and I had anything in common. Everything else fell one side of a line long ago.

What's that like?

Parents splitting up? Better than two people who don't like each other. Two people with strong personalities and loud voices who are never wrong. It takes a while to work out that it's better though. I don't know why. But it's long ago now, and they both worked very hard to make sure that little Alex didn't blame himself for it. As if I'd blame myself. I heard them arguing. The two of them were ridiculous.

Do you see much of your father?

Enough. More than enough. My father's, well, he's a bit of a dickhead. Not in a dangerous way, just a dickhead. In my mother's language he's not a healthy socialising influence. She says he's a stereotype, which he is. Management Man, long hours in the office, lots of travel, family fend for themselves. Even now he's like this weird guy who comes into my life occasionally and asks me bloke questions. Sport, girls, your future. Even superannuation. Once he even started telling me how important superannuation was. What a dickhead. He's like someone you really don't like but you bump into at parties and have to be polite to. And he's such a fascist

146

sometimes. He's so right-wing. I have to tell myself to shut up, that it's not worth getting into the debate. It's terrifying to think that half my genes are his. It's scary enough to think the other half come from my mother. What chance have I got?

My family hasn't always been the way it is, she says after a while. *Not that there were any problems. It was always okay, but I think we all assumed it would always be okay. Then Mum got sick. Maybe we're through that now, but it makes you think of things differently. You hold on much harder, when you used to just assume. It changes the whole family, how the family works, what it means. It's strange. We really thought she might die, but she didn't.*

We walk back along the beach. It's almost empty now, and narrowed by the incoming tide. People have gone for the day, other than a few walkers. At the edge of the sand there are trees with large dense leaves dipping right to the ground.

You see those trees? I say. I used to hide under them, years ago. No one can find you in there. No one can see in. And late in the day there's this incredible emerald light, just before the sun goes down over the hill.

Show me, she says.

And she leads me in, crawling between branches into this small hidden room and the light glows through the leaves, just as I told her. And the leaves tap against each other, flap like green pages turning over in the breeze coming in from the sea.

It's beautiful, she says quietly, brushing her messed hair away from her face.

And she moves her hand to my face and she kisses me on the mouth and I'm on my back on the cool sand

and I can feel her on top of me, feel her back muscles under my hands, her thigh muscles. She leans on her elbows and touches my cheek with her fingers, and my lips, and bites my neck and then kisses me on the mouth again. And I can see her eyes, her pupils huge in the dimming light, feel her tongue, hear her fast breathing.

And the sun is gone, the emerald gone, the leaves a dull green-grey.

We walk back to the house, again holding hands, walking close, nudging into each other.

Later my mother calls.

I'll be up tomorrow evening, she says. *For the weekend.*

I tell her things are okay, that I'm looking after myself.

I eat my dinner in front of the TV.

32

It's as though there's a change in me.

You've brought this about. I'm not what I was.

I can't stand this house when you're not here. When you're here it's a different place. When you aren't it's my past. It's all those other summers. The cricket, the swimming, the long days in the company of people who are now long gone. Like an old writer's early days remembered at some distance, made into a film in the colours of nostalgia. Pride and simplicity and everything out of date. I've seen those movies at the Schonell, *My Father's Glory, My Mother's Castle.* That's what it's like, even though I left this past so recently. What I'm feeling moves in my head like a drug, wild and unreasonable and slow and warm.

My mother talks to me like a voice scratching away at sleep, but I can't hear her for the wind lifting through the broad bright leaves, can't see past your close face.

Tomorrow, tomorrow. She'll be here tomorrow. I must make time for her tomorrow, my mother.

Fortuna.

As if I've ever had this kind of luck.

What happens with you? How long does this last? What do you feel? What happens now? And then what?

Outside you've changed the trees, the sand, the whole coastline.

33

She calls me early.

I've got to go to Noosa, she says. *Do you want to come?*

Yeah. What are we doing?

Taking a load in the ute. Things for galleries up there. On the way home we could swim.

She turns up in an hour with boxes stacked in the back of the ute. I'm on the veranda, waiting already. She sees me when she gets out and she waves. *Hi*, she says when I'm closer, and she makes eye contact only for a moment and tucks a wandering strand of hair back from her cheek.

We get in.

Just throw my towel on the floor in front of you.

We start driving north, and I think we are both wondering how to begin a conversation. She's sitting there, watching the road just as she should, changing gears, taking corners. I'm sitting there, watching the road, watching her watching the road, through the flat brown-house suburbs of Bokarina, Wurtulla, Warana. No one could ever start conversations in these places.

So, what exactly are we doing? I ask her.

Well, we have to see this guy called Lionel. He's got

a couple of gallery shops and he sells Dad's stuff. And we have to go the coast road. My father, this won't surprise you, my father has a philosophical opposition to toll roads, so we can't go that way.

That doesn't surprise me. Mine's the opposite, very much a user-pays kind of guy. I guess that fits too. He showed me a map of the toll road before it was built, and he explained to me its many advantages. I'm still happy with the scenic option.

Fortuna executes the complicated manoeuvre that allows us to avoid the toll road and we work our way through Mooloolaba and Maroochydore and the hinterland cane fields, towards and then past Mount Coolum on the coastal side, the road winding over hills and round headlands and through scrub, past resorts and golf courses and clusters of beach houses and blocks of units with the ocean and the morning sun to our right.

We're meeting Lionel at eleven, she says. So we should be okay for time.

We drive into Noosa from Sunshine Beach, through the roundabout and up the hill and suddenly the sea is ahead of us, slipping in from the east and moving away up the coast in the wide curve of Laguna Bay. We fit ourselves into the tourist traffic and make slow progress towards Hastings Street.

Bloody tourists, Fortuna says, and looks at me and smiles. *They only come here on holidays and they think they own the place.*

If it wasn't for tourists you'd be eating off those plates.

But today I'm not one of them, not moving along with the ambient cool of Hastings Street, like some less cool passenger. Today I'm here on business. Here in an old ute loaded with boxes sitting between a BMW and a

Landcruiser waiting to move through the roundabout. Fortuna winds her window down and turns the radio up. At least the ute has FM, so we're listening to Triple J. Stone Temple Pilots doing Vasoline. She sings along.

We turn into Hastings Street, where the cars move even more slowly as people look for parks.

Nearly there, she says.

She flicks the indicator and when the traffic allows turns right and drives under a building. We park and walk up stairs to street level, past a boutique with a very lonely designer look about it and into the elegant Galleria da Costa. A large balding man with a neat beard and a tropical shirt gives us a wave and walks over.

Oh Fortuna, you've brought a boy to meet me. How nice, he says, giving me a substantial smile.

This is Alex. Alex, this is Lionel.

Alex, it's a pleasure. He shakes my hand. *Come and I'll show you both what I thought we'd do.* He takes us to the far end of the gallery where two of Cliff's plates are on display. *I thought we could do something with them here. What do you think, Fortuna?*

Here would be good. So what do you want, a couple more open and a couple stacked in boxes, maybe with one of the open ones leaning against the ones on top of each other? Maybe some of the grass around it all?

Oh yes. A sort of casual, country, tropical thing. Nodding away. *You have your father's eye, don't you?*

He comes with us down to the ute and helps carry the boxes to a storeroom.

You see, Alex, he says to me, as though Fortuna isn't there, *Fortuna's father is a very talented man. A bit of a rough diamond, but what a gift. I want to be the only person in Noosa who sells him, or at least the only per-*

son selling these wonderful plates. We have an agreement where I pay him quite a lot and he makes them only for me. I have a couple of outlets here, so I think we're both happy with the arrangement. He turns to Fortuna. *Your father's happy with me, darling?*

Of course he is, Lionel.

Oh good.

When the ute is empty and the boxes stacked where he wants them she gives him an invoice. He tells me it was lovely to meet me and shakes my hand again. We leave him looking through the plates, working out which ones to take upstairs.

I think Lionel's always slightly disappointed when it's me bringing things up here, Fortuna says when we're on the street again. *He's got this thing for Dad. He thinks he's very special. And Dad wouldn't even notice, of course. Lionel invites him to gallery openings, as though Mum doesn't exist, and Dad of course thinks those sort of things are for wankers so he doesn't go. And that means Lionel has this idea of him as a recluse, that he's Dad's only access to the outside world. It's strangely romantic. Of course Lionel never leaves Noosa, so he never sees Dad selling plates at the Caloundra markets. For Lionel the world is a very beautiful place between Sunshine Beach and Tewantin.*

And Cliff is a sort of rough fringe-dweller.

Exactly. It's crazy isn't it. But Lionel's a nice guy, and he's good for business.

We stop at Peregian, at a place Fortuna says makes great fish and chips, and we sit on the grass eating off the paper. Around us other people are doing the same, and there are families on blankets unpacking food, a baby misjudging an ice-cream, smearing it across its face and not caring, pointing at birds instead.

I wouldn't have guessed you'd be a fish and chips person, I say to her.

Only sometimes. She smiles. *Special occasions, you know.* And she loads a chip into her mouth with a particular elegance.

My mother's coming up tonight.

For the weekend?

Yeah.

Do I still get to see you? I mean, you should spend some time with your mother, I suppose.

I still want to see you. I'd really be quite happy if my mother didn't come up this weekend.

You're probably not supposed to say that.

No. No. But I want to spend time with you. It's like any time I'm not with you I'm just waiting till I am again.

I'm going red. I can feel I'm going red and my heart is speeding up and I'm feeling a little nauseated. I only just made it to the end of the last sentence, which sounded particularly stupid. Just when I wanted eloquence. She is looking at me, giving me an intense obscure unsmiling look and not looking away. I wonder if she is concerned that I might be unwell.

I know, she says and puts her hand on my hand and squeezes the fingers down into the grass.

We both look at the hands. In this very public place this seems to be all we can do, look at our hands till they make some discreet smoke. I'm squeezing back, she's squeezing, and either we want each other very much or we're arm wrestling. Or the planet has sprung a leak and we're the only people who can save it. The whole moment has the hidden intensity of the look that seemed to begin it.

Let's go, she says. *I want to go.*

So we bundle up the last of the chips and throw them in the bin and walk to the car. And all the time she has a tough, puzzled look about her. She turns the radio down.

Sometimes I want to be somewhere where it's just us, she says. Where that's all we have to think about. Where we don't have to deal with orders for Lionel, or parents, or you and bloody uni.

I've never felt closer to her than right now, and all I can do is watch her. I can't say how much I sometimes want this ideal world of just the two of us. This is ridiculous, out of control, all too much. The low trees pass in a blur, Mount Coolum comes and goes.

Your mother, she says, *has she had other relationships?*

What do you mean?

Since your father.

I don't know.

You don't know? If she did you'd know, wouldn't you?

I guess so. So maybe that's no. Maybe she hasn't. I can't think of anything like a relationship. She has friends who are men, but most of them are married, I think. When people come round to dinner it's mainly couples.

Except for your mother.

Well, yeah. But I'm included now, so the numbers even up anyway.

So you go as your mother's date?

No, I'm just there. She doesn't have a date.

Why?

I don't know.

I think about this. I have never thought about it before.

156

I don't know.

How long has she been single?

Years. It's been quite a few years since the divorce came through. For a while maybe she didn't feel like being in a relationship.

But all those years? I think about it for the first time, trying to make sense of it, and maybe she decided just to look after me. She's focusing on me, and I'm just taking it from her. Maybe that's what's been happening and I've been so busy with school and things, my things, I didn't even know. Maybe she hasn't had a relationship, hasn't even tried, in case I don't cope well. And she's put everything into making sure I'm okay. She said to me once, *Don't let this put you off relationships, what's happened with me and your father. Sometimes they work out, and you never know till you try.* And she hasn't had one since, since she said that a few years ago and it embarrassed me, and I haven't wondered why she hasn't had one since. I haven't even thought about her that way. It never occurred to me that she was single, just that she wasn't married anymore.

Maybe I'll talk to her, I tell Fortuna. Just so she knows it's fine by me. I should spend some time with her.

You should. But you should also spend some time with me.

We stop in at a supermarket at Kawana on the way home, and I buy the ingredients for bread.

Later, Fortuna calls me and reads the recipe over the phone.

Your mother will like this, she says. *It's a good thing to do.*

34

So I make bread, though it doesn't seem like much to offer.

I sift and I mix and I stir and I knead, and I know when she'll be here, round about, and I want it to be baking when she arrives, making the house smell like baking bread. My mother, who perhaps does not receive many gifts, will like this. I hope it works out. I am concerned about the imprecision of aspects of the recipe, such as *until it forms a manageable but soft dough*. I'm not sure I have the expertise to judge the manageability of dough. Still, even if I give her a loaf of bread baked with all the sophistication of a house brick she will thank me and tell me it's the thought that counts. But this time I don't want her to settle for that. I want her to like it, and I want her to have a good weekend. I think that thought has not previously crossed my mind in my entire life.

She will go home after work to change and pack a few things, and she will be here as the sun is setting.

She turns up, right on time and dressed like someone who has just come from the beach. *Hi*, she says, and before she's finished her face has changed. *What's that? The smell?*

Bread. Remember I said I was learning to make bread?

It smells good. It smells great.

She walks to the oven with her bag still in her hand, and opens the door to look.

It's nearly ready. But I shouldn't tell you that. It's your bread. She's pleased. I can tell she's pleased. *So when are we going to eat it?*

I hadn't thought of that. When do you want to eat it?

Well how about for dinner? We could make something to go with it. What do you think?

Sure.

What about pumpkin soup? It'd be good with pumpkin soup, do you think?

Yeah.

I've got some pumpkin up here, unless it's gone of or you've eaten it.

I haven't eaten it.

And I think I've got a copy of Uncle Paul's recipe up here somewhere.

Paul is her brother. He's a lawyer in Sydney now, and his pumpkin soup recipe is highly regarded. She finds it in a cupboard, a photocopy of the recipe in his handwriting on law firm letterhead paper, folded and left in an exercise book with other recipes.

So we go to work, as a team, even though we've never done this before. I start to peel the pumpkin with a very sharp knife, but this means my mother, concerned for my fingers, is unable to do anything but watch me and fidget. I give her the very sharp knife and the pumpkin and I peel potatoes instead. And after simmering and blending and straining it looks like we've made Uncle Paul's pumpkin soup, and while it's heat-ing again my mother cuts pieces of the bread for us to try. It's fine, a lot like warm fresh bread should be. She tells me it's great.

When we're eating the soup, she says, as though it's nothing, *So, how was your week?*

Good, really good. How was yours?

Fine. How's Fortuna? How's that all going? I say nothing. I had not prepared an answer for this. I had concentrated on bread, and besides, I can't even describe it to myself. *I'm your mother, I can ask these questions. You can tell me.*

It's great. We've had a great week.

You like her then?

Yeah. Sure. She's great. I like her a lot. Is it possible for you to keep that to yourself?

She gives me a look. *Of course it is. Of course I can keep it to myself. What big secret have you told me anyway?*

Nothing. There aren't any big secrets to tell, but I'd still like to get back to Brisbane without everybody knowing things in advance. When people say *How's your holiday?* I'd be happier if they didn't already know the answer.

So I'm still not forgiven for the Juliet business?

No, that's not what I meant. I'm just working all this out. I'd rather it wasn't public knowledge.

Okay. I can understand that. Are you coming back for your offer?

I don't think so.

For a while she says nothing. I can see she's trying to work out a diplomatic response.

I think I'll stay here, and buy a paper on the twentieth.

Okay. Is that because you're less stressed about the result now?

160

Well, I can't affect the result now. I think I've finally come to terms with that. And I'd really rather not go through the stress of being there with everyone. I still want the result, but it's not the only thing in my head any more.

Good. I think that's good. That's really good if your perspective's changed a bit on that.

If I get Law, I do Law. If I get something else, I do that and see how it goes. Law would be good, I think, but it's not everything.

I used to try to say that to you.

Yeah, I know. I didn't listen. Anyway, it's what I think now.

You're still going to uni aren't you?

Yes.

Good. You had me worried for a moment there.

Uni isn't everything.

But you are still going?

Yes. I just said it isn't everything.

Right. But it's a good idea. It would be a sensible thing to do.

I know. That's why I'm doing it. Besides, I don't have any other skills. What else could I do? I'm trained to go to uni.

She is eating her soup very slowly, carefully, deliberately, and thinking about every word. Every word she speaks, every word I speak. As though this conversation determines my future.

Everything's fine, I tell her. Nothing's any different from last weekend, or a month ago. My plans are just the same.

You seem different.

I'm just the same.

Good.

So stop behaving as if this is all so weird. I've just been having a good time. Entirely within the law and within the bounds of reason. If I told you every detail, which I'm not inclined to do because you're looking at me like I'm an alien, there is not a moment of which you would not approve.

She nods. *I'm not looking at you like you're an alien, not really.*

I'm still not telling you every detail.

I wouldn't expect you to.

Just the highlights then. The drug taking, the nudity, the ridiculous passion.

No. Keep it all to yourself.

Thank you. Now, what do you want to do tomorrow? I thought we might do something tomorrow.

She stops moving, with the spoon at her mouth. She looks at me, as though I've now said something really insane, as though she's left me for a week and I've lost it completely. She draws away from the spoon, looks at me quizzically. I can feel myself smiling, another one of those involuntary smiles that indicate only discomfort. I can feel that I am expected to say something, something that clarifies my previous unexpected remark.

This is great pumpkin soup, isn't it? is all I manage.

Yes, she says after a while, and goes on eating.

UNCLE PAUL'S PUMPKIN SOUP

$^1/_2$ butternut pumpkin
2 large potatoes
1 large onion
2 chicken stock cubes
4 cups of water
1 small carton of cream
pinch of salt
1 small carton of sour cream (garnish)
passionfruit or chives (garnish)
freshly ground black pepper

Bring water to boil, add stock cubes and pinch of salt. Peel and chop pumpkin, potatoes and onion. Add to broth, return to boil and reduce to very low heat (cover). Simmer until all vegetables are mushy.

Strain mixture and then put mixture through blender/food processor (gradually adding cream) and strain mixture again.

Return to saucepan and re-heat at low temperature.

When serving add a teaspoon of sour cream to the soup and garnish with passionfruit or chopped chives. Add freshly ground black pepper to taste.

35

So what does my mother want to do? She wants to go to Noosa. And I know that if I tell her I've just been to Noosa she'll say, *Let's do something else then*, and that's not the point of this.

I'm eating breakfast when she wakes in the morning.

Where's the paper? she says, still some sleep left in her voice.

I haven't got it yet.

But you're eating breakfast. She looks at me, at the toast on my plate, perhaps even at the *Courier-Mail* that should be on the table, but isn't. *I suppose you can eat breakfast without the paper. I suppose I can eat it without a library book in bed.*

She makes toast and a cup of coffee and sits opposite me, still looking at me. Studying me almost, as though I am breakfasting oddly, as though she's never seen me eat toast before.

We take the toll road to Noosa, a series of long straight lines through the bush, running behind things, behind the beach towns and Mount Coolum. We stop three times to pay.

So how was your week? I ask her, though I think I've asked her before.

Okay, nothing special, just the usual. You go to work, you come home. I played touch on Monday night, between attempts to phone you, of course. The season's just started again, so we were all pretty hopeless. So a couple of us went for a run Wednesday, just around Uni. Well, we didn't do a lot of running really. But you have to ease back into these things.

I probably knew her week would be like this, work, home, touch football, unanswered phone calls. But I'm listening to it now as someone's week, not just disregarding it because it's only what my mother's doing. I don't know how it rates as a week for her, if it was lonely or average, or a week she was quite happy with. I can't say to her is this the week you want? Are you happy with week after week just like this?

I'll be back soon, I think, I tell her. I'll probably have uni to get ready for. Are there any good movies coming on at the Schonell?

I don't know. I haven't looked.

It's been a while since I've seen anything so it would be good to go. Maybe we could go if there's anything good on when I get back.

Before the uni orientation extravaganza takes over?

On the toll road it seems to take about as much time to reach Noosa as yesterday. There's a limit to what I can try in conversation without my mother wondering about me, so there are long silences when I sit back and look out the window. Over the years we have become comfortable with such silences on the drive to and from the coast, I suppose since we live together and see each other all the time. We have comfortable silences at home too. Today I feel more need to talk. I would like to know what my mother wants from life, for herself, and if I'm stopping her getting it. For months now, and much longer really, we've both been trying to work out what I want from life, but she's been static in all this, unchanging, as though I've expected her to be. Now I realise I haven't thought about it at all. She's my mother, and I think it never occurred to me she could be anything else.

I knew she was a doctor. When I was very young and I knew she worked to heal sick people I assumed every mother was a doctor because that made sense. I assumed being a mother meant you'd gone to uni and that you healed the sick, played touch football, held strong opinions which you would defend to the death, and that occasionally, after a long, loud, happy night, you might be sick yourself, and you would treat that too.

Later I realised this was unreasonable, and that I was making assumptions on the basis of gender. Perhaps, then, it can be either parent who has this useful qualification.

In Noosa with my mother we don't stand out from the crowd. We take Hastings Street at a browsing pace and stop for coffee at Aromas. We sit under an umbrella in the heat of midday and nothing's moving quickly. We both drink more water than coffee.

This is great, my mother says. *Like being back on holiday. But this time I'm not sitting here talking about Gina's crisis. You're being very nice to me, coming up here with me today when I'm sure you'd rather be spending time with Fortuna.*

I can still do other things as well.

She sips her cappuccino.

What's she doing today?

166

Getting ready for the markets tomorrow, I guess. She'll probably come down later.

There is a pause. Something is ticking over in her mind while she sits holding her coffee cup halfway between her mouth and the saucer.

You don't have anything to tell me, do you?

Like what?

Anything important.

Like thanks for everything. Like thanks for bringing me into this world and filling my life with opportunities? What are you getting at?

She looks at me, to see if she can see it without directly asking, to see if this mysterious truth might be visible if she looks hard enough. *Look, tell me I'm crazy, but you know the work I do. You know what I come across. Is this all because you have something to tell me? Because you can, you know. You can tell me anything. If there's anything you're not sure about I might even be helpful. You're not in any trouble, are you?*

Trouble. As in the consequence of being naughty or something? What do you mean?

Okay. I'll be specific.

Is that possible?

I'm not, she starts and stops and thinks again. *I'm not about to become a grandmother or something, am I?*

No. Why do you think these things? Why can't any of these things stay my business? As if it's even possible anyway. I've only just met her. Or do you think she's some secret I've been keeping for weeks, and it's only out in the open now that she's carrying my child? You just have no idea.

You were being very nice to me.

And I'm only likely to be nice in the context of unwanted pregnancy? What if I just wanted to be nice? What if I even thought about it and decided to be nice?

You mean it's an effort?

That's not what I meant. I just wanted to do something you wanted to do. I just thought it was about time we did something like that.

Yes. That's very nice.

Nice? It's still nice? So clearly Fortuna's pregnant, right? That's what it means when I'm nice to you.

No. She laughs now. *No. It really is nice. I appreciate it, really, now that I've got over my concerns. I just couldn't work it out.*

We finish our coffee and keep wandering. My mother is drawn into shops by some internal process I don't understand, and she tries things on and seeks some input from me. I think I am a disappointment to her in this. I don't think I'm equipped to play this game. I assume that she is considering buying anything she tries on, but apparently this is not the case. She turns and shows me all angles of one garment after another and I nod and smile, visibly avoiding meaning anything. Every so often there is a purchase, and I end up carrying another bag.

We go past Galleria da Costa and I point out Cliff's plates in the window, arranged the way Fortuna had suggested. In the background I can see Lionel talking with a customer near a table of sea-blue glass vases, his hands showing the flowers that might spring from them, a small spray, a single longstemmed rose. The customer nods, says a few words. They both laugh.

Of course I hear none of this through the glass. The cars move sluggishly past, and the people, families

168

moving by in drifts, manoeuvring among each other along the crowded pavement, through the hot, heavy street air. And all I can hear is engines, and passing conversations.

We stop for lunch in a hot room with a beach view, from our table a beach glimpse. A fan rotates high on the wall above us and whatever air it moves passes over our heads. And they're slow with the water, slower even with the straightforward lunch.

How long does it take to make a couple of foccacias? my mother says as the sweat starts to bead on her lip.

The staff on the tables don't seem to care. They take orders and leave them on a peg and stand in the kitchen doorway looking very cool, looking as though there's no hurry at all. As though they are there for display rather than service, part of some catalogue that sells big black boots and shorts and brown muscles and attitude.

My mother calls one over and asks how long our lunch will be.

Shouldn't be long, he says, in a way that is far more dismissive than reassuring. *We've been a bit busy.* As though our expectations offend him.

This place has a very good reputation, my mother says to me when he goes back to the doorway and forgets us. *I think they're too well aware of that.*

When the food arrives it's okay, but it's no better than that.

I've had enough of this heat, my mother says when she's finished. *Shall we go home?*

In the car heading south on the toll road I wonder what Fortuna is doing. Without her I have been a strange spectator, watching my own day pass me.

36

She turns up in the late afternoon. I hear the Moke coming down the road, slowing, parking. I'm ready with my towel.

I think this is Fortuna, I tell my mother. We'll probably go for a swim.

Don't I get to see her?

Maybe. Maybe I'll let her come up when we get back. But please, behave. None of that pregnancy stuff, okay?

As if I'd say anything in front of her.

You've embarrassed me before in front of other people.

All right, all right. Have a nice swim.

I meet Fortuna in the front garden and turn her round.

Shouldn't I talk to your mother? Just say hello to her?

Later.

And just seeing her is exciting. Seeing her for the first time after a night and a day of not seeing her. I want to tell her, and I want to stop right here and take hold of her, forget about the swim, my mother, Len hosing his front lawn and giving us a wave with his free hand.

So how was it? she says when we're in the car.

Fine. It was fine.

I hope you made it nice for her.

I did. You'll never guess what we did. We went to Noosa. Your father's plates look good in Lionel's window.

And your mother, she had a good day?

Yeah, I think she did.

We haven't talked about where we're going, but we seem to be on the road to Kings. Fortuna glances at me, as though she expects more detail. What the hell, I decide. I'll give it to her.

She was very funny, I tell her. You know she works in the Uni clinic and sees all the student medical problems?

Yeah.

Well, I was being so nice to her she thought I was in some kind of trouble. She got really tense. She even asked if you were pregnant. I've obviously never been nice to her before in my life.

Pregnant? She almost shouts this, and laughs. *Pregnant? So what are we going to call the baby? Jesus?*

I can't believe Fortuna can be so cool about this, but then, she's cool about most things. This doesn't bother her. It only makes her laugh and come out with a line I wish I'd thought of this morning. I like her even more.

We catch a few waves, but this continues to be a summer of unimpressive surf. Perhaps when I was younger the waves were the same size and I was smaller. I can remember summer after summer of great surf. It was probably never like that, just a few good waves here and there across all the summer weeks, but I remember it as something better than this.

Do I get to come in when we get back to your place? Fortuna says when we're driving home.

I suppose so. I suppose we can handle it. My mother does get a bit excitable though.

At a stop sign she gathers her hair into a bunch behind her head and winds a scrunchie onto it. The radio station departs slightly from its usual format and plays Linda and Vika Bull, doing 'When Will You Fall for Me?'. I suppose it sounds country enough to be not too out of place. Fortuna sings along quite unselfconsciously. I'm not even sure that she knows she's doing it. It's one of those things cool people aren't supposed to do, but everybody does. Like talking to yourself, or singing in the shower, or making any bowel gas whatsoever. But maybe this is a measure of how cool she is, that she'll sing when she wants to, and if other people can't, it's not her problem.

I sing in the shower. I talk to myself often when I'm home alone, in a normal conversational voice. Sometimes I even interview myself, as though I've become famous for something. This, I realise, is the sort of thing that only a complete loser could do. I did quite a few interviews after the Juliet story, on account of both the story and the fame it gave me. I was interviewed by several magazines. One of them even ran a Win a Hot Date with Alex Delaney competition, and the 0055 number rang wild with the readers' responses. I think I did some radio and TV too. Creatures of the Spotlight on Triple J for a start, and I can remember at least planning to do breakfast with Helen and Mikey. I think I had some expectation that Angie Hart was going to be there as well. I would have been very cool in how I'd handled that, of course, and worked out just the right way to make my high regard for Frente plain, a way that would have encouraged her to feel some lasting respect for me. I would be funny and clever and the whole thing would go very well. Later she'd call me to ask if I'd ever thought of writing songs, to suggest that we might write together, the two of us and Simon Austin. I even had conversations with someone about doing a novel.

And all of this in my room, by myself, in those protracted moments when it seemed quite hard to study for my last school exams. My desk lamp shining across the same page of the chemistry textbook, while I told the chapter on entropy about how I was handling being in the public eye. Sure it takes away some of your privacy, I told it, but that's a price you have to expect to pay. That's part of the choice you're making.

We park outside the house. Fortuna takes my hand as we walk to the front steps.

Please, I say to her, my mother's here.

This would offend your mother? She holds up our holding hands. *Your mother who thinks I'm pregnant will be upset by this?* Waving our two hands as though the notion is ridiculous. Which maybe it is.

Look, I can't explain my mother. This will not offend her. She'll think it's great. She'll think she can touch me all the time. I'd just be a lot less tense if we didn't, you know?

Oh, so it's your problem, she says, and laughs at me, dropping my hand. *What a boy.*

Inside we talk pleasantly, the three of us. My mother has boiled water for tea in the expectation that Fortuna would come in. She has arranged a tray with a plate of biscuits, a bowl of sugar and a jug of milk. I knew she would do this. I knew she would do something to imply some importance. I don't know if she does it intending to embarrass me, or if she thinks it's reasonable to make it look as though she's having afternoon tea catered. But it could be worse. Another fifteen minutes and she probably would have whipped up a batch of pikelets.

Sit down, sit down, she says, and Fortuna deliberately sits quite close to me on the sofa.

My mother then makes a series of unnecessary remarks that I intend to take up with her later. *So, has my boy been behaving himself then?* Things like that. Fortuna, of course, does not deflect these remarks and will not be unsettled by my mother. She turns most of this into a series of unkind jokes, all of which are directed at me. They seem to encourage each other, and they both seem to quite like my discomfort.

Fortuna turns down a second cup of tea and says she should go to finish preparations for the market tomorrow.

And I think I'll have an early night, she says. *I'm really quite tired.* She looks at me, puts her hand gently on my thigh, turns back to my mother. *It must be the baby.* Said with an unflinching smile.

I think I'm going to die. My mother looks horrified. She laughs, an awful laugh, hoping it's a joke at her expense, looking at Fortuna for pregnancy signs that she knows couldn't possibly be there this early anyway. She laughs again, but again it's more like the sound of a parrot being treated cruelly than anything to do with amusement. And she's staring at Fortuna's loose-fitting T-shirt, as though she's waiting for her uterus to enlarge right now.

It's a joke, I tell her. Because of you, because of you and your ridiculous mind.

And she breathes like a person who has just escaped

from something, and she laughs at the same time.

Alex, you weren't supposed to tell Fortuna that.

It's all right. I thought it was funny.

I didn't mean to offend you.

I'm not offended.

These things do happen. I see them all the time.

Is Alex always the father?

My mother laughs and looks at me. *Not always. I'm sure he's very careful. I'm sure he listens to his mother.*

I think Fortuna has to go now, I say very clearly. She has things to do.

I like that girl, my mother says after she's left. *She's really quite sophisticated. I was never like that when I was her age. I could never have spoken to a boy's mother that way.*

Does it bother you?

No. No, I think I'm impressed. And you're such a cute couple.

And she only says this, surely, because she knows how much I'll hate it, because she feels she can't let it end with unqualified approval.

37

In the morning I show due regard for my mother's comfort with routines. I go out to buy the paper. But when I come back she is ready to go to the markets. I tell her I've bought the paper and she says she'll look at it later.

There's never anything in it anyway.

I think I would quite like it if she went back to Brisbane. I don't know how to negotiate my way through a life that involves both my mother and Fortuna. I feel like a shuttlecock, like I have even less control of things than usual.

And I know I have no chance of talking her out of going to the markets. I foresee a debacle. I am tempted to return to much earlier days of school refusal and rush into the toilet and induce vomiting. I really don't want her to go to the markets, but I have no inclination to vomit either, and I got over the school refusal when I was seven or eight. I can't even remember why I was refusing.

She finds a sun hat with a white-spotted navy band and a bag that will accommodate many purchases and we go.

She meets Fortuna's family and things seem fine until she invites them to dinner. I can't believe she's inviting

176

them to dinner. I assumed she'd go home after lunch, like every other Caloundra weekend. But no, dinner. And they accept. Cliff even says *Can we bring anything?* and offers home-made wine. His family shouts him down.

During most of this I am a spectator, as is Fortuna. And I don't feel quite like any of these people, bits of all of them maybe, but not quite like any of them. I don't fit in with this interaction. I suppose I had expected that I would, that I knew just how this would be, that I was the common element, that there would be a small amount of talk, much of it about me, and then we'd go. This feels like it's nothing to do with me. It suddenly looks like the yuppie woman dealing with the hippie people, and then a friendly adult to adult interaction, and then dinner. Watching it, it all seems very reasonable. I'm not sure why I'd expected it to be different.

My mother takes me on a patrol of her regular stalls. We even buy satay sauce for tonight.

I think I'll get a couple of jars, she says, *and we'll have Len and Hazel over too, if they're not doing anything.*

So what do you think of this family thing? Fortuna says on the phone later.

I don't know.

Neither do I.

Just after six the family thing begins.

Despite everyone's advice, Cliff has brought a selection of his beers and wines, with the '93 lychee present among them. The Boits have brought wine made from grapes, and I can tell Len is not at all sure about Cliff's crate of unlabelled bottles. Within minutes, though, they are both drinking something that suits them and they're deep in an intense discussion about their mutual dislike for development. This is a conversation that lasts more than an hour, and I make sure I visit it occasionally to see how it's going. I still feel like the host, and that seems like a host's job, checking to see that long conversations don't involve at least one party being bored senseless. But they're firing. Len's talking about his parents' honeymoon for a week just near here, when the options for travelling from Brisbane were by boat up the coast to Military Jetty, or a long and arduous journey over unmade roads, with patches of sand that could take a winch to get you through. And they're talking about action, about protest, about badgering the council and anyone else appropriate. *The last thing we want up here's bloody canal developments with streets like Lady Bloody Di Boulevard,* Len's saying and Cliff's going *Too bloody right* and other offerings of rebellious affirmation.

And I notice they're drinking beer from unmarked bottles, and their voices are getting louder.

It is a bit like Guinness, I hear Len say. *Isn't it?*

Gail and Hazel and my mother are talking and I walk up to see if any of them needs another drink.

No, I'm only going to have a couple, my mother says. *I'll be driving back later, remember?* She turns to Gail. *I really don't think I'll be trying Cliff's lychee wine. Is that going to be a problem? It seems important to him.*

Gail laughs. *He'll be okay. His life is full of disappointments. He'll survive if you don't try the wine. Most people don't. I just tell him I can't because of my medical problems. Just mentioning that sort of thing makes him uncomfortable. Once I told him what a kidney biopsy was like and he went white and fell over. So I don't have to try the wine now. He made Alex drink some the other night, and Alex was so nice about it. People usually spit it out, but Alex drank it.*

It's really not that bad.

It's awful. It's all right to say that it's awful. Deep down Cliff knows it.

At the far end of the veranda, Cliff has a wine bottle open. Len is holding a glass of clear liquid up to the light and speaking quite earnestly about it. I can only catch an occasional part of his verdict. *Lychees, who'd have thought it?*

179

Fortuna, I think, is watching all this the way I am, but to a less neurotic degree. Both of us feeling that the combination of people is a little unlikely, both of us hoping it will work.

Skye and Storm stick with each other, sitting in a dimly lit corner drinking water, whispering and smirking as though they know something that confirms the rest of us as idiots.

Dinner is ready and my mother declares it to be a *help yourself sort of thing.* The satay tastes great, and having helped her to make it it now seems really quite easy. She waves her empty glass at me and sends me downstairs for more wine, more of the holiday red that she keeps under the house in the box it came in. Each summer a dozen cheap reds and a dozen cheap whites, kept down there where it's far too warm and they won't last. But they're not supposed to. They're for nights like this, nights when people drop over and wine seems a good idea. My father, who believes he has taste in wine, brings his from home when he comes up here, from the shelf in his garage he refers to as his cellar. And he bores me about each bottle and keeps them in the bedroom cupboard, where he says it's cooler. And when my mother turns up with her two dozen he sucks his teeth and shakes his head and says, *Tessa, don't you have any friends who actually like wine?*

When I get back upstairs Cliff is lounging in a bean bag in an almost horizontal position, drinking precariously and talking about music. He declares Fleetwood Mac's Rumours album to be one of the top ten of all time. Only I know what this means. It means my mother becomes excited, shouts *Yes! Yes!* and sends me back under the house to find the old seventies turntable and records. When I carry these inside she's sitting on the edge of Cliff's bean bag, drinking red wine and joining him in singing a medley from the album.

Play it, play it, play it, she says to me, flapping her free hand to speed me up.

I play it, she sings along, Cliff sings along, Gail sings along. I can't believe this is happening. I can't believe my mother is part of this scene too. She can't sing at all but she's shouting along and I think she's drinking quite quickly now.

What about going home? I say to her. You were going after dinner.

She flaps the hand again to shut me up and in an instrumental passage tells me she'll go first thing in the morning. As though this is nothing. As though she does that all the time.

Len, having had a few drinks and usually keen for a bit of a sing, picks up the album sleeve since it has the lyrics on it, and joins in.

Fortuna, seeing I have been stalled by this madness, comes and sits next to me and gives me a glass of wine.

Parents, she says, and shrugs her shoulders. *What would they know about music?* She laughs, and I don't know if she's mocking me or them.

I'm past caring, or understanding. I drink the wine.

Cliff persuades my mother, now in a more experimental frame of mind, to try the '93 lychee. It puts a confused look on her face as she works out how to respond once she's tasted it, but then she goes and gets ice-cream from the freezer and a large bowl and several spoons, and everyone is invited to try it as an ice-cream topping.

And I think we're all shouting now, shouting and not

listening. All except the twins, who find this incredibly boring. They come and talk to Fortuna, but I can't keep track of what they're saying. She's nodding. They go to my room and I don't see them again. The singing goes on, long after we run out of ice-cream. I tell my mother I can't go downstairs for more red wine, because I think I can't. My bladder is very full and I go to the toilet and I am not confident when I get there, not at all. I sit down and the toilet walls move around me quite quickly. So do other things on the way back to the lounge room.

I feel good, I feel really good now. I sit on the sofa and sag down into it in a state of great immobile comfort. Fortuna joins me and says, *The twins have gone to bed. They figure nobody's going so they've gone to bed. Is that okay? In your bed? Is that okay?*

The complex broken jigsaw of a smart answer bumps across the edge of my mind but I end up just nodding.

I think I hear the Boits on the stairs. I think our parents keep singing. I think Fortuna moves in very close to me and kisses my left ear and then falls asleep partly on me but in a way that restricts my breathing only slightly.

39

It's light when the noise wakes me. The thumping of drawers in a different, closed room.

Fortuna's arm is across my chest. We seem to be locked at the ankles. My head feels quite untidy and I think I have had difficult dreams.

I disentangle my feet without waking her and move her arm to her side. She breathes like a person deeply asleep, face down with her head turned away from me, her crumpled shirt pushed part of the way up her back with our slow slide off the spongy sofa. For a while I just watch the bare skin of her lower back.

The thumping goes on. I hear my mother's voice as she talks to herself in the bathroom, and several squirts of a nasal spray. She emerges looking quite tired and with two Beroccas in her hand. She sees I'm awake and she signals me to come over. She pours us each a glass of water, but the Beroccas both go in hers. She swirls them round and watches them fizz, and seems to forget I'm there. I stand next to her drinking my water, wondering if I'm supposed to speak first. She keeps swirling, leaning on the bench with her left index finger supporting her pale, furrowed, uncomfortable brow and swirling. When the Beroccas have dissolved she signals me to follow her outside onto the back veranda.

She leans on the railing with her free hand and looks out through the trees to the sea. She doesn't look at me. She talks quietly.

Remember years ago, that talk we had. Do you remember? Well, if it's time to do the things we talked about, in that talk, I'm not saying you have to do anything, or that you have to not do anything, cause it's not up to me, but I'm just saying, do you remember? Do you remember what I'm saying? What I'm saying now.

Yeah.

This is not the moment to point out that she has a serious tense problem. This has the look of another one of those parent things, where they just can't get to the point, all metaphor and memory and mutual discomfort.

And when she says *that talk*, I can only assume I know which talk. I can only assume she doesn't mean the talk that began with, *I've thought about it and I want you to know that if you told me you were gay I could come to terms with it.* When your mother has no idea about your sexual orientation, and you certainly haven't been trying to hide it, you must be on a pretty bad losing streak. I also decide she doesn't mean the talk that began, *I went to an Adolescent Medicine seminar today and one of the speakers said that if your adolescent child is alone in their room with the door shut they're almost certainly masturbating.* It took an effort to adjust to studying with the door open, but I managed.

I expect the talk from years ago to which she refers is one of the girl–boy talks.

And she's still going while I'm half-listening, still

184

rambling around it, whatever issue it is that's troubling her.

Well, probably all that I'm saying is that, you know, I know what happens. I know how things work, okay? And if you have any questions, or anything, I hope you can ask me. I hope you can feel okay about asking me.

Yeah.

You feel okay about asking me? If you have any questions?

I feel okay about asking you. At the moment I have no questions, but I've got your number, if that happens to change.

Good. And other than that, I suppose, there's not much to say, is there? She pauses. I have no reason to contradict her. *So have a good week, or however long you're here. Please come home soon, or sometime, whenever you're ready, but hopefully fairly soon. Talk to me, phone me sometimes and talk to me, and we'll all be hoping that whatever's in the paper later in the week it's okay by you. And other than that, other than that, it's probably important to bear in mind that you should buy the ones with the lubricant and with the semen reservoir at the end.* We're both looking out to sea now. Neither of us has any hope of surviving eye contact while my mother talks about my intimate bodily fluids. I can't even tell her she's missing the point. *And with nonoxynol-9 because you can never be too careful. That sounds awful, but it's only the responsible thing to do, to be careful, and there's no need for anything flash, no fancy colours or ribbing or anything. But the main thing is to make sure it goes on early and goes on properly.* Freeing her right thumb from her glass and rolling her left thumb and index finger down it, but in a

185

way that seems subconscious, like she's done it a thousand times. But maybe only with that very thumb, as an unnecessary demonstration to one nervous student after another. *And make sure there's room at the tip. Okay?*

Okay.

Good. She smiles now. The ordeal is over for both of us. *She's great isn't she? She's great.*

We go inside. She finds her purse and gives me fifty dollars.

This is for, well, all that, she whispers, pointing back out to the veranda and then doing the thumb thing again. *To help with being careful.*

I think with fifty bucks I can be incredibly careful. What do you think I'll be doing for the next few days? Do you think I never get outside?

I have to go now, she says. *I have to go to work.*

I'm not really happy about you driving like this. You don't look well.

I'm fine. I'm just a bit tired, but I'll be fine.

Call me when you get to Brisbane, okay?

She smiles, as though this small display of caring makes her very happy. She obviously has no idea how bad she looks.

40

She goes before anyone wakes.

I decide I can clean up some other time and I lie down again next to Fortuna and she stirs only slightly, says *Hi* and sleeps again.

I think we all sleep for another hour or so before the twins wake us.

You're still being very boring, Skye says, jabbing an index finger between my ribs while I'm still in a dream. *You were very boring last night and you're still very boring now. My sister only likes you because she's very boring too. Get up please.*

She and Storm each take one of Cliff's arms and lift him off the bean bag. He looks around this unfamiliar place as though he has been carried somewhere in his sleep.

Oh, Alex. Hi, he says, and sits down again.

Dad, Skye says in a way that should be making it clear to him that he too is boring her.

What, there's no hurry is there?

So the day proceeds without hurry.

Gail wakes with the noise of people moving around and a little more dignity than the rest of us were allowed. No finger in the ribs, no twin on each arm.

Fortuna starts toasting bread and I boil water for tea and we sit out in the cool breeze on the front veranda with our breakfast, not saying much. Soon the twins agitate to go home.

I might stay, Fortuna says.

So the others leave in the ute, and as they go Cliff calls me over to the window and says, *She's great, your mother. Bloody great, isn't she?*

And they drive away.

So now it's just the two of us. Just the two of us and maybe the whole day, and I'm really not feeling well.

I think I need to lie down, Fortuna says. *I think I need to be somewhere not too warm and not very bright and where I can lie down.*

So we open the front and back sliding doors and shut the curtains and the screens and turn on the fan and we lie back down on the sofa in the calico-filtered light. And the fan blows old smells of satay and wine and warm air and the curtains flap up from the doors and fall back again, and it's too warm. Too warm today to feel well, too warm to feel well on a saggy seventies sofa when every part of your body seems to be succumbing to a degree of seediness.

I'm glad you stayed, I tell her.

Yeah, she says. *Me too.*

And our faces are close but neither of us moves to make them any closer, to do anything. My mouth tastes like kitty litter and my teeth feel like they're wearing socks. And she's looking at me with those green eyes. She touches my cheek with her fingertips and she says, *I've got to sleep.* And she holds my hand again, and her eyes close and I watch her up close till I sleep too.

In the afternoon Len Boit comes over with half a water-melon, a machete and a few poems.

Felt a bit rough earlier, he says. *Thought there was a chance you might've too, so I thought we could all do with some melon. And then I worked out young Fortuna had never heard any of my poetry.*

He sets himself up on the old veranda table and lops off a few semicircles of melon. Fortuna and I settle our-selves into the white plastic chairs as Len readies himself against the rail, straightening his glasses, shuf-fling his papers, peering through the sheets to find the right poem to start with.

Here we go, he says. *One about having a bit of a headache the morning after.* And he's off.

Several poems, several different themes, most des-tined for the Humorous section of his next book. Fortuna and I listen and laugh and discuss when discus-sion seems the appropriate response. And we sit back spitting seeds far beyond the veranda down onto the carpet-grass lawn.

Then he says to Fortuna, *You might remember your dad and I were talking about Caloundra and what it was like a while back. I've got a few about that too, about*

189

when I was young.

And the place might be very different but the poems are still about beaches and surf and fishing and sitting back not doing much. He reads one about the *Centaur*, the hospital ship torpedoed off Caloundra in 1943 and tells us he was away then serving overseas. It was a time when not many people lived in the area and few came on holidays, and there was a fort at the north end of Bribie Island.

I must have walked past it, I think. Years ago when I went over on my surf ski and walked through to the coastal side of the island, and there in the dunes and lantana were concrete slabs and broken-down build-ings. I never knew it was a fort. I never knew that any war had come this close, that there were soldiers there, and heavy guns, ready for enemy ships at sea that never came. But there were other sides to this, as Len tells us, rhyming his way through 'Boys of the Eighth Heavy', a long poem about dances at the fort when the Caloundra girls were shipped over wearing their best to meet the soldiers of the 8th Heavy Artillery, and they burned dried cow dung to keep away mosquitoes. It's all so dif-ferent, the music, the clothes, the threat of invasion. Just thinking about it I can't imagine it happening anywhere near here, and particularly not so recently that people can remember it. Fort Bribie. It's hard to believe it now.

From our back veranda the sea does not look like a place for war.

We finish the melon and Len gets to the end of the poems. He goes home and we swim, not a wave-catch-ing swim, just walking down to the sea behind the house, over the hot sand, into the water. Just us here.

We hose the salt off each other when we're back in

190

the garden and we sit on a low tree branch with our towels around us, our wet skin picking up the smallest of breezes and drying cool.

This is good, you say in a voice no louder than it needs to be.

There are no noises near us, just the unfolding edge of the quite peaceful sea.

And right now you're all that's on my mind.

The shade and light fall around us, over your face and shoulders and legs like a mosaic, small shapes of shade and light, the sun passing through all the angles of the she-oak canopy.

Your lips are cool but your mouth inside is warm and wearing what we are my arms are on your skin, your sea-washed smooth skin. And the sun lights your eyes like deep green seas, and your wet-straw hair. And your skin is against mine, soft against mine.

We don't talk.

We spread our towels between the trees, vivid rectangles of colour on the sparse grass and sand, the swaying tree-shade. We lie on our backs looking up through the branches at the deep blue sky. We curl towards each other, face each other. As though there's no one else, as though the only place that matters is here, beneath these trees. The tide comes in up the beach. We sleep again, and wake when it's cooling down. All uncomfortable on the hard ground.

This is another day ending. It's the seventeenth. January seventeenth. Time is shortening. Our time. I want to tell you I'll have to go soon, back to the city, but that's not the end. That I'll be back here, with you, on this grass, the first chance I get.

Again you leave me at the beginning of night. Me with the empty house of the past and the long hours with no one. I walk up and down on the seagrass matting, feeling more hours leaving. Wasting and leaving. The TV plays summer repeats, but I'm not listening.

On the eighteenth we go to Bribie. We take the surf skis from under the house and load them in your car and set off from Golden Beach, over the drifting sandbars and the oystered outcrops of rock and the deep dark band of the water of the passage. We pull the skis up onto a narrow beach and walk until we find a path.

I remember walking here years ago, having paddled here the first time on the ski, setting out by myself from the other side of the water. Taking several summers and then weeks to decide I might get to Bribie and back, weeks to find enough confidence. And when I landed it was as though I had reached another country, one that had not been visited for a long time. And I found something in the mud, sticking out of the mud like an old Roman sword, and I walked through the mud to get to it, not taking my eyes off it in case it would disappear, in case I wasn't seeing it at all. I imagined taking hold of this old blunt blade and drawing the sword from the mud and carrying it back on the ski, taking care of it across the deep engulfing waters of the passage and the sand-bottomed shallows. Walking from the water, the sword in my hand, telling my mother I think the

Romans were there, on Bribie.

And it didn't disappear and I took it in both hands and the mud gave it to me with a shlock and closed over the hole with ooze and the hilt of the sword was the skull of a pelican, the blade I held its beak. I washed it with care at the edge of the water and took it home anyway, all the time wishing it was something else.

I found a pelican's skull just near here once, I tell you. Sticking up out of the mud.

We follow the track among trees and I wonder if it was cut in 1943. Or if the tracks from the war are long gone and grown over, and people walk new tracks between new trees, and the tracks move like the sand-bars in the passage, following lines of least resistance. Closing over with growth, opening up with death again, a bush dying, a tree dying and drying and falling in the harsh salt sand. I can hear the sea ahead of us.

The path leads us to a concrete slab, and the sand comes over one corner of it in a slow wave. And there are holes like square-cut wounds where metal posts have rusted away, orange stains around the edges, the last of the metal crusting in some of them like scabs. There is glass across the concrete, the smashed glass of stubbies thrown hard against it, brown beer glass scattered across the slab. We stop and look at this, as though something might happen.

It's the fort, isn't it? you say. *Part of the fort.*

Probably.

And the sea sounds close, as though the next rise is the only thing that stops it from sweeping over this outpost. We keep walking and the track takes us through thinning trees and scrub and onto dunes. There is a concrete building at the end of the track, at the edge of the beach. Its doors and windows are just spaces and the warm wind skates off the sea and runs through these spaces like the low noise of breathing, like a long breath out.

To the south the beach goes as far as we can see. Some distance to the north the island ends and across the water is Caloundra, Bulcock Beach, Kings Beach, the headland, covered with red-roofed houses and brick blocks of holiday units.

I've been here once before, at least near here. A few summers ago, with this same view. I remember the Keneallys had cousins visiting from interstate. We came across from Golden Beach in boats. I crossed the island with one of them, north of here maybe, different paths. I think she raced me over here. She challenged me and we raced along a path ahead of the others and I caught up with her among the trees and stayed just ahead all the way to the sea. We walked in the edge of the surf and she splashed me, started chasing around me. And I told her the beach wasn't safe here, wasn't safe for swimming, that her uncle had said the sand slips away from you and people have been swept out to sea.

And she kept saying, *The others will be here soon, the others will be here soon,* as though something had to happen before they arrived.

She was twelve, I was fourteen. She had a body only just beginning to be female. She was a child so I thought what's the hurry, what's the problem? *The others will be here soon.* Repeatedly, splashing me with some mad urgency. And now I think I know. She was splashing me and telling me time was short and the next move was up to me.

I splashed her back. She was twelve. Nothing else

195

occurred to me. I thought she was just splashing. But when I splashed her back it seemed to annoy her.

The others appeared at the end of the path, and the splashing stopped and we walked with them, up and down this foreign beach with a view of Caloundra like a postcard. I found a piece of wood the size of a fist that had obviously come from a boat and she asked if she could keep it.

She told her parents we had found it, the two of us when we had been alone on the coastal shore of the island, even though that wasn't quite true, and I think she took it home to Melbourne with her. She must be fifteen now.

But I don't tell you this story. I don't tell you any of it. It just flicks into my mind briefly and only stays long enough for me to think I've worked it out.

I'm older now. This is our beach. Neither of us needs this story, or anything stolen from another summer. It's not important enough.

We've got to remember where the path was, you say. *We shouldn't go too far.*

We walk in the sea almost to our knees and the broken waves run past us and up the white sand. I look down at my feet in the clear water, sending up puffs of sand as I walk, and the foam of the breaking surf sucks back to the sea, holds my ankles for a moment and then lets go, swirling away.

You're not saying much, you tell me. *Is it the uni thing, the offers the day after tomorrow?*

Yeah.

And maybe it partly is.

Yeah, I'd be lying if I said I wasn't thinking about it.

I put my arm around you and you swing yours

around me. We walk more slowly, less steadily. I kiss your hair and it tastes like salt.

I want to tell you how you've made the uni thing a little less important. How today is manageable, and it might have been much worse. I expected to be back in Brisbane now, festering horribly, being very hard to live with but refusing all the time to talk about it, or admit that it mattered. It matters, I can tell you it matters, even if it's not the sort of thing that matters to you.

This is our beach, you say. *No one else's. We could do anything here.*

We turn and keep walking, still at the water's edge so the beach is still unmarked, as though we've just landed here, come out of the sea. We could do anything here.

We're facing the town now, walking facing the place where I've spent every summer of my life, but looking at it from far away, as though it's not quite real, an image picked up from somewhere else by a trick of the sun and dropped in front of us like a mirage, a whole silent town left at the end of this beach.

People arrive, a family with a large cool bag and a beach umbrella. A football sails up into the blue sky and thumps down onto the sand not far from us. Two boys chase towards it as it rolls to a stop.

We are back at the concrete ruin, back at the track. You lean against the southern shaded wall of the building and look down at the beach. The concrete is cool where the sun hasn't touched, never touches. The ball goes into the sky again and this time lands on the water of a receding wave. It wobbles from side to side and another wave takes it, lifts it and pushes it up the beach. One of the boys scoops it up and runs.

You put your arms around my neck and shrug as

though you don't care about them, as though they can have the beach now, and you say, *Oh well*, and you kiss me on the mouth. I close my eyes and hold you through your salt-matted hair.

On the nineteenth you say you'll keep me busy. You say you can tell I'm more tense. You tell me you're getting tense for me now and you never thought you'd be tense about tertiary offers.

But of course there's more to it than that. The nineteenth puts me a day closer to leaving.

I talk about school, because I can't talk about leaving. But I also can't stop talking about school. I can't seem to help it, just like the day we met, when you laughed at me for waiting. Waiting for something I'd have to wait sixteen days for. Now it's tomorrow.

We go to Kings and the waves aren't bad but there are too many people. And in one way I want tomorrow to come right now so I can get it over with, in another I don't want it to come at all. In Brisbane they might already be setting the type for the paper, setting the letters together for my name and whatever outcome I'm entitled to.

I phone my mother at lunch time when I know she'll be home. She seems careful with the conversation, as though she doesn't want to say the wrong thing. So I do most of the talking. I tell her Law isn't everything, that I don't have to get into Law to be worthwhile, that I'll survive, whatever the result. And today I wonder if I believe any of this, or if it's just words, chanting along beneath the fear of failure and not meaning much. She goes along with it, says it's all good, but I can tell she doubts that I believe it.

We go to your house in the late afternoon. Cliff calls me mate a lot, and says I should stay the night. Skye unfolds a table tennis table and insists that I play, as though she's being nice to me. But of course she plays table tennis the way I imagine Jean Claude van Damme would if he really didn't like someone. She strikes the ball with a ferocity unlikely for her small arms, and it is clear her main intention is to hit me as many times as she can. When I'm fifteen-twelve ahead she cracks the last ball and we stop. She is visibly annoyed with the flimsiness of table tennis balls, now lying around her like the shells of several smashed eggs.

We eat dinner and I sleep by your bed, on a mattress on the floor, with you looking down on me from the edge of your pillow.

It'll be okay, you tell me, *whatever happens*, and you reach down to hold my hand.

You sleep and your hand goes limp and your fingers uncurl passively.

I don't sleep. For a while I lie looking up at the ceiling. I can hear almost nothing, no cars, no waves. Just the conversations of insects, the breeze circling through the tops of the trees and your soft breathing. A creak in the next room as someone rolls over in bed. A possum dropping from a branch onto the tin roof, somewhere over the far side of the house.

I rearrange my pillow and I sit with my back to the wall. I watch the moon on you, coming through the window and falling across the white sheet that covers you, the hills and valleys your body makes in this grey-silver landscape. You lie facing me, your left leg bent and your right leg straight, the sheet dipping between them, rising over both of your thighs, curving up over you and across the high plain of your back, lifting and falling with the rhythm of each breath. And from the top emerge your T-shirted shoulders, your bare arms, the gentle empty face of sleep and your hair catching the moon in a way like fine-spun glass.

So I hardly think about the paper at all. I watch you. I think about you. I think about the two of us in this room, the shape of you under the sheet, moving only slightly to breathe. Only I can see this.

I wonder what will happen, since we aren't the same in many ways. What will happen when my result is out, when I have to spend some time in Brisbane again. At this moment, when I'm with you, it's easy to know what I want.

I sleep on and off, and I feel good each time I wake. You're still there.

You wake when it's light, and then you wake me. I hear you saying my name, softly as though it's still part of some great dream. But of course I'm not the sort of person who has great dreams, so I should know better.

It's that time, you're saying to me with your face quite close over me and your hand on my shoulder.

You say you'll make me tea but I don't feel like tea. I need to know.

The others are still asleep when we drive to the newsagent. It's probably just after six when we get there and you pay for the paper and I run outside with it, opening it across the bonnet of the Moke, looking frantically for Delaney AP, Delaney AP.

There are a lot of names, too many names, I have to turn another page for the Ds.

So, you say beside me, *is it there?*

I find the Ds. I find the Delaneys, all ten of them. I find Delaney AP. And course code 708001. Arts/Law, Queensland Uni. I'm in.

43

I call my mother, I call my father. It's early but they're both up, both with the paper, both wondering when they should call me. I don't tell them any attempt would have been futile. I can't face explaining the details of a night spent elsewhere.

My mother's excited. I can tell. I think she's bouncing up and down when we talk. She cries briefly, or at least her voice changes in a way that makes me think she does. She denies it. She says it's her sinuses playing up. She says my grandparents will want to celebrate this too and how about dinner on Saturday, anywhere I want, she'll book it today.

I could come up after work on Friday, she says, *and bring you back down on Saturday.*

I could catch the bus down on Saturday.

Of course, whatever you want, but you will come, won't you?

Of course I'll come.

My father sounds excited too. This is a sound I'm not used to, so I'm only guessing.

I was already awake when the paper came over the fence, he says. *I've been sitting here with it ever since. Isn't it great? I bet Tessa's proud of you too.*

You've done well.

Thanks.

I want to do something. Can we do something?

Sure. What sort of thing? I'm going out with Mum on Saturday night.

Okay, how about Sunday? Could we do something on Sunday?

Sure.

Okay, now, I've got an idea. It's up to you, it's completely up to you and if you don't like it we'll do something else, but this is my idea. It's Ben's birthday next Thursday, so what I'd like to do, and this is really selfish of me so tell me if it's a problem, if it's not what you want to do, but what I'd like to do is to do something for both my sons on Sunday. I'd like to have a party for your result and for Ben turning two. And I'd want your mother to be there, and your grandparents, and anyone else you wanted. Now, if you don't want that we can have Ben's birthday next weekend.

No, it sounds good.

Really?

Yeah, really. It sounds good.

When the call ends I remember a one-sided conversation we had when Ben was born. When my father came to school in the middle of maths in the first week of year eleven and I thought someone must have died. He hadn't slept all night and he went on and on about the appalling details of the labour since he hadn't been in the room when I was born and he had no idea of the horror of it, and he took me somewhere near school for lunch and I couldn't work out why. And he said to me, *Alex, I look at you and I know I've let you down. I don't know why, I don't know how it all happened but I know I've let you down. And I want you to know that I know that. And I also want you to know I'll do better this time. I'll be there more, I'll be more involved. I'm learning from my mistakes. I want to be there for you too, if you ever need me.*

And I think I said thanks in the most hollow and contemptuous way that was reasonably possible, and now I think I wish I hadn't.

Now when I get into uni he doesn't know if he should call me. He lies awake waiting for the paper and he sits with it for a couple of hours, proud of me but unable to call, unable to take the risk of telling me. In case I say thanks that way again. Thanks and leave my life alone and you'll never stop paying for your mistakes.

I bet Tessa's proud of you too. That was as close as he could get, that and a desperate idea to get his sons together.

I think I thought I meant nothing to him.

But at the end of the day it's just us.

At the end of the day the phone calls are over and it's just us on Moffat Headland at the top of Queen of Colonies Parade. We swam and you chose to come this way back from Kings and we stopped at the crest of the hill. I don't think I've ever stopped here before, even though I've spent all my summers close by. I've looked up at the headland from beaches, I've driven past it, but I've never stopped just here.

And there's a sandstone pandanus stump carved with the name Queen of the Colonies, and the story in brass of the ship's boat that was driven onto these rocks in a storm a hundred and thirty-two years ago next April. *And the survivors were marooned for fourteen days*, it says, *living on shellfish and berries until rescued by a search party from Brisbane.*

And all my life Brisbane has been less than an hour by road. There has been no reason to contemplate life and death and shellfish and berries, just a dull drive up a straight road with two lanes each way. Even the name of the boat seems so old. Queen of the Colonies, part of some lost empire.

I'd never even thought about the name of the street

before. It had always just been there.

The sun will set soon. In the south-west, beyond the next headland the Glasshouse Mountains stand in a hazy blue twilight, like people lost in fog.

In two days I'll be gone. The day after tomorrow I'll be catching the bus and then I'll be in Brisbane, doing family things, seeing my friends. I'll be trying to keep every moment of this in my head, and I'll be planning to come back as soon as I can.

And you don't want to talk about this either. So inside me there's a strange small glow of satisfaction when I think of the paper, telling me what I wanted it to, but there's also a feeling that I'm being cheated of something.

I have to go back, I say, more because the words are in my head than because I mean to. But Caloundra's close.

Yeah, I know. Make sure you remember that. When you're a law student and all sorts of other things are happening.

So we sit on the grass looking south, down over the beaches and across to Bribie. And the cicadas screech in the bushes and cars pass on the road above us.

I want to stay with you tomorrow night, you say. I have to go home soon, but I want to see you tomorrow and I want to be with you till you leave. Okay?

Yeah, good. Stay at my house you mean? The two of us.

Yeah.

I lie down, with my head on the cool thick grass and I look up at the purpling, darkening sky. There are no stars yet.

You sit still looking south with the breeze touching

the ends of your hair and your legs crossed and your hands playing idly with the taller stems of the grass, working them into plaits and then undoing them again.

Your lips are moving, and on the breeze I can hear you sing in a whisper, bits of 'Not Given Lightly' from my Frente EP.

It's never been more apparent that it's a love song, about the choice you make to take your feelings and give them to someone.

It's a good song and even in a whisper you do it well.

On the twenty-first I start the day with a swim, like any other holiday day. Down at the beach early, just me and the waves.

I'm a law student now, or about to be. I wonder what this means. I wonder how smart they'll all be, all of them school debating champions with big plans. Or maybe at least some of them like me. People who aren't really sure what they want, but thought this all seemed like a good idea at the time.

My mother has already said, *You're in and that's what matters. Pass and enjoy yourself. This is a time when you're supposed to have fun.* My father of course phoned back to give me his views on the opportunities for Australian corporate lawyers in Asia and the Pacific rim. He has such big hopes for me, but they just aren't mine. I listened, I think politely. I even tried to show some interest, but I'll have to be careful not to show too much.

And you've ducked under all this, slipped away from the attentions of QTAC and TEPA and any other tertiary entrance acronyms. You've got plans of your own, plans of art and waves and honey. And for you this isn't brave. It's quite normal. For me, the bravest I can be is to pick a variant of the safe option, do the law degree and maybe something I like, literature perhaps, with my BA. Something my father would see as useless and my mother as interesting, in a hobby kind of way.

But the waves don't know I'm a law student, and I still surf like a nerd king, with high levels of both competence and unattractiveness. What you see in me I still don't know. I don't know how we got past that first conversation.

And I don't want to go to Brisbane tomorrow. Just out here, in the water, thinking about it, I feel in some ways like an unjustly condemned man planning his last day.

I want to cook you dinner tonight, when you come over to stay. I want this night to work. I strip the sheets from the double bed my mother sleeps in alone, and I fit a clean set. All the time thinking that we might spend tonight together in this bed. My body next to your body all night. And I'm changing the pillow slips, turning the sheet down, and every mundane moment excites me. Who sleeps on which side? Who determines these things? I can't believe I'm just making a bed, and I'm expecting this.

Len takes me to Coles to buy ingredients. On the way back we stop at the bottle shop and he insists on buying me an expensive bottle of white wine to congratulate me. I don't put up much of a struggle and he says, *It should go well with dinner.* And he asks me if I've got everything I need. For a moment it concerns me that he's about to become the second person this week to give me condom money. Then he says, *You know, fancy wine glasses, candles maybe, that sort of thing. What do you reckon?*

You come over late morning and you bring a bag

with a change of clothes and a toothbrush. You show me the toothbrush and you laugh and say, *This seems like a strange thing to bring, a very grown-up thing, but my father said just because I was staying the night here didn't mean I should forget about my dental hygiene.*

You take it to the bathroom and put it in the spare hole in the toothbrush holder and ask me where you should leave your bag.

So I tell you, Anywhere you like really.

You look around and walk into my mother's room and drop it at the foot of the double bed.

Do you want to go for a swim?

We cross the garden and the beach and swim in front of the house. The midday sun gleams on its white-painted fibro walls and dazzles across the tin roof and leaves slabs of black shade under the veranda and the trees. The water is a perfect temperature and we lie around in it just beyond the breaking waves.

I wish you weren't going, you say to me.

I'll be back. I'll come back all the time. And you can drive to Brisbane too.

We get out when our fingertips are well shrivelled and we shower and walk up Seaview Terrace to Moffat Madness, the world's least appropriately named eating place. There must be some irony in it for someone. Every time I've eaten there, usually with my mother, it's been a place of calm, magazines and board games and very sane food and no sense of hurry.

We order toasted sandwiches and milkshakes and the tanned white-haired man chats to us in a friendly way that seems far from mad. One day I'll ask where the name came from. Maybe it's something to do with the reckless way the tanned white-haired man decided to use his superannuation package, setting up a sandwich bar at Moffat Beach. If so, it's a very functional kind of madness. I can see him preparing the toasted sandwiches, and he's even handling the avocado meticulously.

We sit at the table near the door.

So what's happening on the weekend? you ask me.

Family stuff. Dinner tomorrow night with my mother and my grandparents, her parents, probably at a place called Portofino at St Lucia.

What's it like?

Portofino? My mother likes it. The service isn't quick so it's not a great choice if you're in a hurry. They make possibly the best garlic bread in the world. It's on a thin crispy pizza base and it's quite oily and loaded with garlic. Then I'll probably have the bucatini matriciana. My grandparents will have lasagna or ravioli. They get annoyed with anything you have to wind onto a fork.

And all the time I'm saying this I'm realising you won't be there. I want to tell you that I'll miss you, I want to stop now and tell you how I feel about you. I'm looking into your eyes and telling you about my grandparents eating Italian food, and I think you mean a lot to me.

My mother? I don't know what she'll have. But she'll be quite excited and toasting my future repeatedly with whatever wine she's bought. And my grandparents will ask me questions about studying Law, and I won't be able to answer them because I don't study Law yet. Then Sunday we'll all be over at my father's during the day for the Festival of the Sons. He's keen to let everyone know we're both important to him, I think, so Ben's birthday and my uni offer are going to get equal billing.

210

That, knowing my father as a man of limited style and imagination, will be a barbecue with a table full of salads and bread and him in the back yard talking about the Weber as though it's a scientific instrument. But I'm going to be nicer to him than usual, even if it's not easy. After all that I suppose I'll start to catch up with my friends, people from school. I'll be going to uni with some of them too.

What are you going to tell them?

Tell them?

About this. About the last few weeks. They'll ask you what you've done these holidays. What are you going to tell them?

And you're smiling as though you're in some way taunting me.

I don't know. I really don't know. I haven't worked it out. What I'm going to tell them. I think I'd like to tell them nothing. I'd quite like to say that it was just the same as every other year, and then listen to the lies they tell me.

46

In the evening you take a long shower while I'm starting to cook and you come out wearing the dress you brought. And today we don't go to a hilltop to watch the sun set into the hinterland, we don't go out for any big view. We stand on the back veranda and we see the sky and sea darken, change into their evening colours, merge into blackness. And the moths and Christmas beetles bounce against the kitchen windows trying to get in to the light.

And there's a breeze, finally a breeze to begin to end the heat of this day.

You reach your dark arms out to me and we kiss till the cicadas are quiet and evening is gone.

My father, you say, *you should have seen him. Gripping onto the toothbrush and telling me about dental hygiene and being careful.*

And of course I've been through this scene myself, but with a clay penis instead of a toothbrush.

Being careful seems to be an important topic, I say. For him, for my mother, for Len. They're all very much in favour of being careful.

Can we talk about that? All of that?

Sure.

You nod, and plan what you're saying. *I want tonight to be really good. I don't want any added pressures, not that I mean pressures from you. What I mean is the pressure of anything big and different. Anything I have to wonder about when you're gone. I want to be with you all night. And I don't want to have to deal with anything else just yet.*

That's fine. That's good. That suits me too, really. I'm not in any hurry. This is really good, all of this. I don't want to make any kind of mess of it. I don't mind letting it take time.

But not forever.

No.

Soon maybe.

Soon could be good. As long as we make very sure we're careful of course.

Clean our teeth and things.

Yeah. My mother gave me fifty bucks for things.

That's a lot of things. Boxes of twenty four were nine-fifty in a pharmacy in Bulcock Street earlier in the week.

Cheaper in Coles.

She laughs.

I'm glad you're staying. That's what I want. Really. What I don't want, what I couldn't stand, would be to spend my last night in this house here by myself, with you so close by. I want to spend every minute with you till I get on that bus. And of course that's the sort of thing I can't tell my friends. That's why I think I'll tell them nothing.

What do you mean?

I can't tell them what I feel. They're my friends. They'll expect any story to have certain predictable parts to it. I can't tell them how I feel about you. The stories they like would be more in terms of What did you do to her? How far did you get?

Good choice of friends. So what will you tell them?

That I caught waves, watched the cricket. I don't know. It doesn't matter. Tonight none of that matters. That's a Brisbane problem. I don't want Brisbane problems tonight. Tonight no pressures, no problems, okay?

We go inside. The bread will be brown by now, the soup simmered enough.

And every time I look at you tonight I have a crazy idea that I'll come up here in a week or two and turn down Sunset Drive and there'll be only bush, and I'll never know whether you're there or not, and I'll never find you. Pushing deeper and deeper into denser and denser bush, calling your name and not knowing if you're hiding from me or just not there.

We eat by the light of beeswax candles. I watch you dipping your spoon down into the thick yellow soup, breaking the steaming bread with your hands.

This is really nice, really good. I didn't know you cooked like this. I didn't know you made things.

So I watch you eat the things I've made for you and when we've finished you say, *Let's go down to the beach.* And we take the rest of the wine and our glasses and sit on the sand. And there are lights on Moffat Headland, blocks of units and the streetlights of Queen of Colonies Parade, and the sky is full of small stars but the beach is a dull glimmering silver-white and no one can see us here.

You sit with your arms around your knees and your glass in your hand, looking out at the invisible sea. There is a ship going past, a line of white lights that must mean a ship, far away and moving slowly south.

214

And maybe they're watching the shore, the lights of Caloundra, but only to keep far enough away. Up and down the east coast doing routine trade, container ships carrying everything a ship can, cars, refrigerators, furniture, and in no danger of coming to grief on these rocks, starving and scared and hoping for rescue. I wonder what this beach was like then, when the boat from the Queen of the Colonies was wrecked here, before the sand had started to creep through the beach-house gardens, all the time still chased by the sea.

The tide, I think, has reached its height and turned. I pour the last of the wine into our glasses and we drink it.

I'm getting cold, you say, and we go inside.

We lock the doors and turn out the lights and you say you can attend to dental hygiene later. I open the windows in the bedroom and a breeze winds round from the sea and comes through the screens.

You lift my shirt up and over my shoulders and head and I feel the air on my back. You kiss my chest, take my face and kiss my mouth. I undo the buttons at the back of your dress and it slides down over your shoulders and drops to the floor. You stand there for a moment without moving, with the streetlight across your body, your white bra, your brown skin. We lie on the bed. Tonight you don't have the sheet on you, you're not wearing the T-shirt. I kiss your thighs, the tops of your breasts, I put my hands all over you and you hold me and close your eyes and your breathing deepens. You turn to face me, turn me onto my back and kneel over me, your hair catching all the light. You pause, as though you're not sure what happens next and then you lower your face down to mine, you balance on your elbows, tuck your hair behind your ears

215

and you kiss me on the mouth.

And for hours it's like this and you say to me, *Sometimes I want to do more,* but we don't.

We fall asleep next to each other, holding each other, our heads on the same pillow, one white sheet over us, lit up by the streetlight outside.

In the morning when the sky is a vivid blue in the window and the rosellas are shrieking in the trees I'm lying on my back, my head off the pillow, looking up at the seventies raffia shade over the light on the ceiling. And you've pulled the sheet around yourself, turned away from me and drawn the sheet with you so I'm lying covered by almost nothing. I move in against your sleepy-warm body and put my arm around you. You take my hand and bunch it in with the sheet against your breasts, but you don't seem to wake.

I sleep for a little longer with my face against your shoulder. My hand feels your heart beating slowly when I wake again. This time you wake too and you open one eye and see me and say, *Oh.* You move so that you're on your back and looking at me with both eyes.

When I get up I make tea and bring it back to you and you're propped among pillows. And your dress is still on the floor where it fell, and my shirt, and you take the tea with both hands and sip it slowly.

Later we swim, and we both know it's the last time for now. You take me out along Sugarbag Road and we have lunch with your family on a big outside table under

217

a tree. Cliff paces up and down and looks at the ground and tells me to come back soon. Tells me not to waste my voice and all my other talents, but he never makes it clear what they are. He gives me a tape of the final mix of 'Caravan of Love' and a couple of other things, and he says he'll teach me how to play guitar one day, if I want. *Cause I hear you're making more bread than a bloody bakery now*, he says and smiles.

Skye hugs me and we both go very red and pretend it didn't happen, and then she's rude to me again.

You drive me to the bus and we don't say much.

You park the car and the bus is already there.

I have a couple of things, you say, and you reach for a box in the back. *The first is from my dad. It's called The Potter.*

And it's a tiny clay figure of a very feral looking man wearing only a vest, reaching out to a small wheel with big mad hands.

It looks like it's got three legs, I say.

You look at it closely.

That's my dad, you say. *Underneath it all a very ambitious man. The other one's from me.*

It's a grass head the size of a golf ball, and it's got my ears and it's laughing, and its body is a small jar done up like an academic gown, with Little Alex written around the base.

It's a one-off, you tell me, as though you need to. *A Big Merv just didn't seem right. It's just an undergraduate at the moment, but if you water it enough the grass grows till it becomes a mad professor.*

Just for a moment, holding these things in my hands, I think I might cry. It's a very strange and unexpected feeling.

I open my bag and wrap them carefully in T-shirts and put them near the honey you gave me when we first met.

I wrote some poems, I say, and I hand them to you.

Oh. I didn't know you wrote poetry.

That's all right.

You look at the first one and start to frown and blink and tell me you'll read them later, at home.

And could you take my library books back? I never got around to it. I think I only read one of them anyway.

You take the books from me and laugh. It seems like such a domestic task.

Next you're going to tell me they're overdue and I have to pay a fine.

I hadn't thought of that. I can pay you back from my condom budget. Soon.

I feel mildly nauseated when I get on the bus, quite unhappy when it drives away, past the car park you've already left, an empty space someone else is already backing into.

The bus is not even half-full and I have a double seat to myself. I put on my Walkman. We head out past the drive-in where the markets will be tomorrow for the second-last time, out past the airfield and the new developments and the race track, heading for the highway. At the other end my mother will meet me, other things will begin.

I play the tape, and I hear myself singing 'Caravan of Love'. I sound more confident than I felt. Then your voice comes on, explaining what you're doing, that the next two songs are just you accompanying yourself on guitar. And you sing 'Not Given Lightly' and 'Bizarre Love Triangle'.

And I play these songs over and over on the long straight road south through the pine forests and past the mountains and into Bald Hills and the north of the city.

I'm thinking about uni, what it all means. Sandstone buildings, drinking, exams twice a year. But I can't fit myself into this yet. But I don't fit into those twelve years of school either.

Just these last three unlikely January weeks.

What critics have said about *After Summer*:

"Very little escapes Earls's gentle, sardonic but tolerant view of human nature. This is a genuinely witty book."
Pam Macintyre, Australian Book Review

"A stunning novel … This is one of those books that reaches all ages, a beautifully written, poignant tale of adolescent angst … a little gem of a read."
Frances Whiting, The Sunday Mail

"Nick Earls's *After January* has reminded me what it is like to fall intensely, and requitedly, in love for the first time … *After January* has, I think, oodles of credibility."
Nicola Robinson, The Australian

"A fine, subtly tuned story of a young man's three weeks on the brink of change in a sharply drawn world."
Sally McInerney, The Sydney Morning Herald

"An important new voice."
Agnes Nieuwenhuizen